Outstanding Praise for Trevor Scott

"A damned good writer."—David Hagberg, bestselling author of *High Flight*, *Critical Mass*, and some 70 other mysteries and thrillers.

"*Strong Conviction* is a good crime story with interesting characters and solid writing. Trevor Scott weaves a web of small-town controversy that entraps our hero...with vivid description he paints characters who breathe and sets up believable conflict."—*Pine Bluff* (Arkansas) *Commercial*

"*Strong Conviction*...a first class shocker fully developed with crystalline and lively dialogue, adroit pacing, and commanding characters who find themselves enmeshed in extraordinary and often deadly circumstances, with the right mix of potent romantic interest."—*Scribesworld*

"Mr. Scott brings his powerful and prestigious experience into play with his newest thriller, *Hypershot*. Mr. Scott utilizes his usual arsenal of literary techniques to build *Hypershot* into a first-class thriller: pacing, effective love interests, compelling characters finding themselves in unusual and deadly circumstances, clear and effective dialogue, and just plain thrilling circumstances. His settings are reminiscent of James Bond. A great fourth book!"—*The Midwest Book Review*

"Previous titles have fit the Tom Clancy techno mold, but this topical tale of DNA research and a possible cure for heart disease falls more in the James Bond tradition of fancy cars and fast women."—*Publishers Weekly*, on *The Dolomite Solution*

"Trevor Scott delivers with *The Dolomite Solution*. Scott ratchets up the action. He is an expert at thoroughly deceiving the reader, drawing us into a seemingly insolvable plot just as he fascinates us with action that is non-stop...a wonderful read."—*The Midwest Book Review*

"Scott has the high-tech jargon down pat...he takes readers around the world for a thrill-packed adventure. Technothriller fans looking for an alternative to Clancy will find Scott a somewhat smaller-scale but perhaps even more authentic alternative."—*Booklist* on *Extreme Faction*

"Trevor Scott's action-packed post-Cold War spy thriller is certainly that-a thriller. *Extreme Faction* takes the reader around the world, into different cultures, lifestyles and ideals with flawless ease. I'd recommend this adventure highly."

—*Duluth News-Tribune*

"*Extreme Faction* is fast-paced, realistic, and more than a bit frightening."—*Statesman Journal*, Salem, Oregon

"*Extreme Faction* is a thrill-packed, non-stop, absolutely riveting action/adventure, novel from first page to last."

—*The Midwest Book Review*

"As much fun as a Bruce Willis action movie."

—*Rocket eNewsletter* on *Extreme Faction*

"A great read. A roller coaster ride of murder, espionage and intrigue."—David Hagberg, author of *High Flight*

"*Fatal Network* is a masterfully written, splendidly executed, superb thriller."—*The Midwest Book Review*

"This is a thriller with some real thrills, an adventure with new ideas, and an espionage drama firmly rooted in the convoluted realities of modern Europe. A real gut-buster of a thriller."

—*Statesman Journal*, Salem, Oregon

"Unique twists and turns...a deadly cat and mouse game."

—*Duluth News-Tribune*

The DAWN of MIDNIGHT

Also by Trevor Scott

Fatal Network
Extreme Faction
The Dolomite Solution
Hypershot
Strong Conviction

The DAWN of MIDNIGHT

Trevor Scott

Salvo Press
Bend, Oregon

This is a work of fiction. All characters and events portrayed in this novel are fictitious and not intended to represent real people or places.

THE DAWN OF MIDNIGHT

Salvo Press
P.O. Box 9095
Bend, OR 97708
www.salvopress.com

Library of Congress Control Number: 2003102336

ISBN: 1-930486-39-1

Printed in U.S.A.
First Edition

CHAPTER 1

MUNICH NIGHTS

As the tour bus cruised through the Bavarian hills, Karl Schwarz flipped from thought to thought, unsure of what he should do, not certain if he should act on an impulse as primal as death or life, but infinitely aware that to do nothing was unacceptable, tantamount to defeat.

He gazed out at the full moon, bright and glowing off the soft, snow-covered fields, and envisioned hunters huddled in their little wooden boxes high above the edge of those fields waiting for unsuspecting game to wander from the groomed forests. Shots would ring out in the clear brisk darkness, echoing from dorf to dorf through the dull, hollow air. A clean death was all that mattered. Humans hoped for as much.

The bus swept westward along Autobahn Eight toward Munich, with each curve of the road obscuring Karl's view of that precious moon. His mind fluttered by with the frozen trees, and he wondered if Angelique was awake at that very moment in her own bus, distracted by the snow in Switzerland. Her long spiral curls, visibly auburn even in the darkness of the bus, flowing over her blue ski jacket. Her green eyes piercing the mountain peaks like lasers digging for diamonds. He became lost in his own reflection. His eyes were large and close set, between a short nose that had been broken once in a downhill race, but showed little sign of it. His dark, long hair was a disheveled mess from his hat going on and off all day. He needed a shave, an act he hated, especially on cold days. So he often remained that way, with a bristly beard that his mother would say made him look like a bum. He didn't have time to worry about such trivial things. Life was moving far too fast and he couldn't keep up.

The skiing tour was nearly over. St. Anton, Innsbruck, Stubaital, Kitzbuhel, Kaprun. An hour ago in Austria the bus had crawled along like a paralyzed rabbit through a Tyrolian pass, obscured by thick heavy snow, and Karl thinking the slopes would be perfect powder in the morning. With snow, as in life, timing was everything, and he could only wonder just how nice the Zugspitze would be by nine the next morning. Not that he could do anything about it.

He reached down, rubbed his sore right knee, which he knew was filling up with fluid by the minute, and he longed for the trainers of his past. He would sit and drink a beer while the man stroked the balm over his knee, the heat unbearably pleasant. The pain was almost constant now, especially after a day of skiing or simply being in the cold.

He glanced over his shoulder. Nearly everyone was asleep, tired from a half-day of skiing and the long bus ride.

The bus hummed along in the slow lane. Not many cars came flying by, Karl noticed. The snow that was already blanketing the Alps was sure to push north to Bavaria soon.

Fritz, the bus driver, hunched over the large steering wheel, rocking his head slowly to the sound of Mozart's Eine Kleine Nachtmusik emanating from speakers on the dash of the plush Mercedes bus. He was dreaming of the next time he would have sex with his girlfriend, a large-breasted Fraulein who could carry eight, liter-mugs of beer at a time at the Hofbrauhaus.

The bus slowed for the outskirts of Munich and then turned off the autobahn. A soft yellow glow hung over the city, as if it had just been bombed and burned to the ground and was now smoldering in dead silence.

Knowing they were getting close to their hotel, people stirred in the back of the bus. The streets were nearly vacant, as they were arriving far later than expected due to those high mountain snows. The bus rounded a corner and pulled over in front of the Kaiser Hotel. It was a three star place the tour company used for short stays.

Karl picked up the microphone and hesitated a moment before pressing the button. "Ladies and gentlemen, we're at our hotel," he said, his voice deep and resonating to the back. "What a ski trip. Seven days, seven nights. And only one person airlifted out. Not bad."

A few people in the back laughed.

Karl continued, "On behalf of Bavarian Tours, we appreciate your coming along on the most fantastic ski trip we've ever catered. The snow was great. Wasn't it?"

There were a few soft words of affirmation. Most people were looking for their hats and gloves that had slid under their seats.

Fritz turned on the blinding overhead lights, bringing groans from the half-asleep.

And now the part Karl hated most about his job. It felt far too much like begging, he thought. Yet he appreciated the extra money. "Much of my livelihood depends on the kindness of friends like you," he said, as he always did in his most solemn tone. "If you feel compelled to part with a few leftover Deutsche Marks, since you will be departing the country in the morning, Fritz and I would cherish the gesture."

Fritz leaned his thick arms over the steering wheel and gave a slight laugh, his robust gut wiggling up and down. He knew the tip would never come his way. But the company paid him well for his services, and Karl always bought him a beer or two with the money for the use of his name.

The tired tourists streamed slowly off the bus dropping bills generously into an open ski hat on the dash.

When they were all gone, had pulled all their equipment from under the bus and shuffled into the hotel, Karl finally scooped up the hat and the money. He wouldn't count it until he reached his apartment. He never did.

Fritz closed the lower bins outside and got back behind the wheel. "We could get the bus back and go for a beer," he said to Karl. It had become a ritual. Finish the tour, drop off the bus, and go for beer.

"Sorry, Fritz, my man. But I'm supposed to meet someone at the Zanken Bar."

"Angelique," the driver said. "I just heard over the radio they'll be another half hour. The snow in Switzerland was worse than Austria."

Karl checked his watch. "Could you drop me off?"

Fritz smiled and pulled out into the light traffic of evening. In a short while, he edged the bus to the curb and opened the door for Karl, who promptly stepped down to the sidewalk.

"Don't forget the meeting tomorrow," Fritz called after him.

Karl gave a thumbs up and then skirted into the bar.

The Zanken Bar was smoky and dark. Crowds of people hugged the long wooden bar, cigarettes propped from the sides of their mouth's and their eyes squinting from the contrail of smoke, with heads bobbing the affirmative. Tables were full, empty glasses stacking up like crystal towers of decadence.

Karl got a beer and found a lone table in a corner with only one chair, sat down, and watched the people. It was a mesmerizing ballet of microcosmic simplicity. Here was a young couple with more problems than they would ever admit to each other. There was an old man who had fought hard in the World War, downplaying any indiscretion of youth as the times had surely dictated, standing with a son who neither understood those times nor cared about them one way or the other.

In his reverie, Karl almost missed her coming

through the door. But there she was, scanning the room for him. Angelique Flaubert was wearing tight black ski pants and an aqua blue jacket. Her dark hair was held back from her face with a head band, with spirals curling back over her shoulders. But it was her eager eyes, those jade windows of a troubled soul, that seemed to zero in on him like radar to a heart that beat louder than any other in the room.

She smiled and headed toward his table, stopping only to pick up a spare chair.

Karl rose and they shared kisses on each cheek. Then they sat, inspecting each other for changes, even though it had only been a week since they last saw each other.

"Quite the snow storm," Karl said.

A waitress came by and set a beer in front of Angelique, like an automatic response. Woman comes through door, sits down, gets beer.

"I guess we come here too often," he said to her.

She smiled and took a sip of beer, licking a drop from her full red lips. "We almost had to spend the night in Vaduz," she said. Her accented words lingered in the smoldering air like tidbits of sultry lyrics.

"A night in Liechtenstein," Karl said. "Sounds like a porno movie."

Time seemed to slow down.

Karl leaned across the table and put his hand on hers. "So I say to this guy from Dallas: 'You've skied before?' He says, 'yeah.' Turns out he'd gone to Taos one weekend, and probably hung out on the bunny hill."

"Are you sure he peed his pants?"

"Absolutely," Karl said. "Two days later the guy takes a half gainer on a black diamond run. Broke his damn back."

"Airlifted out?"

"Yeah. They took him to the same Innsbruck hospital they brought me six years ago."

Neither said a word for a long while, content with simply watching eyes blink, chests heaving with each breath, maybe the occasional dimple of smile. The sounds all around them were a meaningless verbal collage.

She broke the silence. "I had this couple from London who insisted I take them on difficult runs at Grindelwald."

"Not again. You didn't send them. . . ."

"All the way to Wengen."

Karl laughed. "Send a bus for them?"

"Of course. After a few hours."

"You're cold. What'll you do with your time off?"

"Paint. Todd wants to go to the gallery. My parents want me to go home this weekend. Plan for the wedding."

Karl took a long drink of beer, watching her carefully over the top of the mug and wondering how he should deal with that. Luckily, the beer would speak for him.

"You can't go! Your interest in Adrien rivals mine for ignorant, obnoxious tourists with too much money and zip for brains."

"You've never met Adrien," she said without vigor. "Nor will you."

"You don't want to go to Brussels. Stay here. We'll have sex all weekend."

She frowned. "We've never had sex."

"Not that you know of."

"I think I'd know."

"Oh, you'd know."

Angelique got up and went to the bathroom. While she was gone, Karl found a couple of cigars at the bar. He lit both of them and brought them back to his table.

When she sat down, she accepted a cigar and brought the end to a bright red.

"This is all I need," she said.

They sat back in their chairs trying their best to send rings of smoke into an already cluttered atmosphere. He was unsure if times like this would hold some meaning to her when they were forced to part ways for good.

She flicked some ashes into an empty beer mug. "Where'd you get these?"

"Some guy at the bar."

"I think I'm getting sick. I just want to go back to my place and take a hot bath."

"Now you're talking."

"Alone."

"Can I at least watch?"

She snubbed out the cigar and got up to go. Karl was thinking about doing the same thing, but he decided to keep his cigar as the two of them left the bar.

•

After walking Angelique home, Karl made it back to his apartment building two blocks from

Goethestrasse, limping badly now but feeling little pain. The moon brightened his path through the metal gate along the brick walk to the old wooden door.

On the inside door there was a note from his landlord. He tried to read it in the obscured moonlight streaking through the glass on the door, but couldn't. So he stuffed it into his ski bibs and started upstairs. Good news never came from his landlord. At least his rent was paid this time.

He went up the narrow stairs in the somber darkness to his third floor studio apartment, jangled his keys free from his pocket, and aimed it for the lock. The key flicked about at the lock going everywhere but in. Finally, he opened the door.

Clicking on a small table lamp, he scanned his tiny apartment. There was a small kitchenette to the right, the bed against the wall where the ceiling slanted sharply with the pitch of the roof, the ragged sofa that the landlord owned, and his bike against another wall. His fedora was propped over the post at the foot of his bed like one of Queequeg's heads ready for sale. The dark oak walls were brightened with posters Karl had acquired from various ski resorts and cities he had toured. Nothing too permanent, for he knew how fluid life could be. The large window was the highlight of the room. It had bordering lead glass on three sides, and he could look out over a park to watch couples kiss and children play. He didn't have to go far to observe life.

Everything seemed in order. His landlord had a disturbing tendency to move freely through his place when he was gone on longer tours. His friend

Todd had seen him coming from the place on two occasions.

He took in a deep breath. Stale beer perhaps.

He cracked open a window, letting in the cool freshness of snow and the sounds of the street.

After his shower, in sweats now and bare feet, he plopped down on the tired brown sofa and savored the first gulp of a cold beer. He pulled up the right leg of his sweat pants and squeezed a few inches of balm on his knee. The distinct odor of eucalyptus and menthol tweaked the hairs in his nostrils, making him sneeze. He would have to tend to his own pains, his own anguished past. The pain would pass soon with the balm, but he thought now of the day his knee snapped, plunging him, hurtling him down the side of the mountain. He sucked down more beer.

He had been too young for one Olympics, peaking while still in high school. He was first in the state of Minnesota in slalom and giant slalom. But slalom was his specialty. It wasn't a great accomplishment by some standards. When he went to college for a while on scholarship in Colorado, his teammates questioned if Minnesota even had skiing.

Perhaps it had been that desire to prove himself that ultimately led to his accident. He wouldn't have thought that himself, in a sport that measured success or failure in less than a second and where injury lurked on every turn, but his passion, nonetheless, had been labeled by others as fearlessness or recklessness. Only one would ever know the truth.

Karl opened another beer and then stroked his knee gently. He pulled the Deutsche Marks he had received as a tip from his ski bibs and sorted the bills by denomination. More than he normally received. Fritz would drink well after the meeting, he thought.

He slid his laptop computer closer to the edge of the coffee table, flipped the cover up and logged on. Having dreamt of a story on the moonlit bus, he had to get what he could down quickly. For that's how his mind worked. A dream and then frenzied work. It was as if he were on a tight slalom course. He studied the gates in his mind until he knew every turn, every dip of the mountain, and then when it was his turn to hit the course, it was all over in a few minutes. Revisions were like his second and third runs. Refinement.

He had only the meeting to attend at noon tomorrow at the headquarters of Bavarian Tours, so he could afford to stay up and get a good start on his short story. His novel would have to wait. He stared at the blank computer screen and could think of nothing. He glanced back at the fedora on the bedpost. It wasn't much to look at really—a soft brown felt with a dark nylon ribbon and a subtle bow at the left side. He turned his eyes back to the blinking cursor, but then was drawn again to the hat. There was an intangible power to it, begging him to pick it up, imploring him to caress it and gently prop it onto his head. He had felt its power before, and knew that he was stupid to believe in such things. He knew that it had to be nothing more than a rabbit's foot. Yet, he was enticed once again, standing before the brown fedora, reaching out for it. He relented. He sunk his hand underneath it, lifted it from the post, and blew off the dust that had collected in a week. Slowly he brought it to his head. Gently he slid the fedora onto his wet hair. It was a perfect fit.

He sat down on the sofa and looked at his computer screen again, and then he typed away quickly now, his fingers clicking as fast as his mind.

CHAPTER 2

ANGELIQUE

It bothered Angelique to simply drop all of her ski equipment on the wooden floor of her apartment, as she had before going to the bar to meet Karl. Yet, some things were more important. Now she was too tired to unpack, re-wax her skis, clean the dirt from the crevices of her ski boots, and prepare her clothes for washing. Instead, she tried to ignore the temporary mess as she heated water on the stove for a cup of tea and then went to the bathroom to draw water for a hot bath.

Back in her living room, with the kitchenette off to one side, she hesitated and scanned the room. There were plants everywhere that would need water. She had soaked them prior to leaving for Switzerland a week ago, but she knew the heat from the old radiators would have dried them out by now.

She filled a watering jug in the kitchen sink and quickly made her rounds to her children, giving each a healthy drink.

"I'm sorry I've been gone so long," she said softly in French to no plant in particular. "I'll be home for a week and give each of you a bath tomorrow."

She brushed the dust gently from the dull, heart-shaped leaf of a philodendron.

She had thought about getting a cat, but she was gone far too often on tours and would have had to neglect it or entrust its care to someone else, who would probably forget about it. Besides, she always had Todd on the floor below to talk with, and a cat seemed pathetic for a young woman in her mid-twenties. A cat was for widowed grandmothers. And there was Karl, enigmatic Karl.

Looking out through the window at the dark English Gardens, she thought about how the sun would be perfect later that morning. She preferred the morning light, especially when the flowers in the Gardens were in full bloom. Todd liked the evening light, where shadows cast their darkness into a somber ambiguity. She was Monet and he was Delaroche. Karl was Michelangelo's theme.

Just as she finished watering the last plant, the tea pot started whistling. She hurried over to the stove, scooped the kettle to another burner, and turned off the hot one.

She poured the hot water into an old cup she had purchased at a flea market a few months ago. It was hand painted Bavarian china, cracked like the road system of the northern Alps.

As she headed toward the bathroom, she stirred an herbal blend around in the cup. The water in the bathtub was nearly to the top, so she quickly set her tea on the window sill and shut the water off.

Next she methodically undressed. She always started from the top and worked her way down. The sweater, the turtle neck, the bra. Then she looked at herself in the full-length mirror. She had lost weight in the past few days. She lifted her breasts up. They were firm, but not large. The nipples had become hard from contrast between the cool room and the warmth of her clothes.

She slid her stretchy ski pants over her hips, flipped them to the floor with her foot, and then removed her long underwear and undergarments in one quick motion. She gazed at herself again. She was proud of how she looked now, athletic yet soft. As a child and a teen she had hated her body. She had been skin and bones. Most of her friends had developed early, had numerous boy friends because of that, and had experienced sex before finishing school. She, on the other hand, had never found men very interesting, since they hadn't given her much consideration. Until recently.

Thinking about her fiancé, Adrien, was less than stimulating. He was, after all, someone who was chosen, not someone she would have selected. She quickly vanquished any thought of him as she slipped into the hot bath.

She was overwhelmed with the power of warmth. Sliding down lower, she totally immersed her head underwater. Then she slowly emerged and wiped her long hair to the side of her face. She took a sip of tea, set the cup on the ledge again, and gazed into the flowered print on the cup's side. She worked the bar of soap over her body, across her breasts, and down between her legs. She closed her eyes.

When she was done with her bath, she dried herself, put on undergarments and a long cotton shirt, and went directly to bed.

As she dozed off she thought about Karl again, wondering if he was up right now typing away on his computer, the fedora propped on the back of his head.

•

It was a bright, clear December day when Angelique and Karl decided to go for a drive east to Marienbad in the Czech Republic. Angelique had heard of the Christmas market through a friend at the museum, and Karl had always wanted to go there to see what Goethe had found so lovely, other than Ulrike.

They took Karl's car along the winding country roads of Bavaria and Bohemia; roads that could have been straight if it were not for engineers with automotive foresight.

Having arrived in the famous spa town at noon, they went immediately to the flea market in Goethe Square. Covered booths were snuggled in tightly, each selling something different. Tree decorations at one, candles at another, and anything from expensive antiques to cheap curios at various others.

Karl had spotted the tea cup sitting on a table among old brass lanterns and hand-painted plates. It was like something she might have found in Brussels, but of higher quality. The cup reminded him of a few his mother and father had, covered with dust and never used, stacked high in their China cabinet. There were red and blue flowers along the outside brim, and at the bottom was the Bavarian inscription. It was like his father's relatives had made over a hundred years ago in Bavaria. Angelique had accepted the gift graciously. She liked those things that others were never likely to have.

After drinking a warm glass of wine and eating curry wurst and French fries for lunch, Angelique came across the fedora. She knew immediately that it was old, but wasn't certain just how old. When she first picked it up from the bottom of the box, her fingers seemed to tingle, and a strange sensation spread throughout her body until she became chilled. Without saying a word, she gently placed the hat on Karl's head and gave him a thorough inspection from front to back. Somehow the fedora fit him perfectly. Not just the size, but it seemed to match him, become a part of him. Karl's hair stuck out from the back and appeared to curl up around the brim. He smiled, not certain how he looked.

It wasn't until they had returned to Munich and were having a beer at the Steinhaus that they realized how special the fedora could be. The hat didn't look like much really—a fawn color, with the darker ribbon and crumpled bow to one side. They had the impression that the hat was merely a castoff from a bad 1940s movie. But then Karl had noticed that the leather sweatband was relatively new, compared to the rest of the hat. When he peeled the band back, it revealed a second leather band that was worn from many years of going on and off a man's head. It was hard to see the embossed stamp on the right side, considering the dark lighting of the bar, but Karl couldn't take his eyes off of it. He brought the hat to his eyes for closer inspection. Sure enough. It was there. The inscription read: *F. Kafka.* The lettering had been gold at one time, but was now chipped away in various places and faded.

Angelique was immediately impressed. It was a sign. Fate. She believed in such things. Fate determined what each person became. Fate and fate alone was decisive in every human endeavor, so why try to change things? Instead, people should base decisions on what they felt deep within themselves to be the truth. That way they would never walk through the forest aimlessly, but with an innate compass bearing true to their soul. She had known all along that the hat, the fedora, was special.

Karl was skeptical from the beginning. When Angelique said the fedora would give him strength and power as a writer, he simply smiled and sipped his beer. It was a fedora after all. Nothing more.

CHAPTER 3

THE HOFBRAUHAUS

Karl woke to the sound of traffic on the street below his building seeping in through the open window. He was curled up in a ball on the sofa, his ski bibs pulled up over his bare shoulders for warmth. He noticed the fedora had fallen from his head and was crunched into one corner of the sofa upside down, as if looking for donations.

He swung his legs to the floor and kicked an empty beer bottle into two others lying under the coffee table. “Shit!” He checked his computer to ensure he had saved the story and logged off. He had.

It was eleven and he had a brutal headache. If he hurried, he’d have enough time to hop a train to the meeting.

He pulled on black jeans and a dark green shirt, wiggled into his black loafers, and then swung on his leather jacket, slightly worn at the elbows. Angelique loved the jacket, so he wore it every chance he got. He picked up a photograph from his nightstand. He and Angelique stood arm in arm on a mountain overlooking Innsbruck. Her long hair flowed back over her shoulders in the wind, a glint of ruby. Her crisp smile glistened in the sun as if God had positioned the rays precisely on her rosy cheeks. The photograph was only a few months old, but was already marred slightly from handling. He set the photo back in its place and positioned it precisely so he could see it while lying in bed.

He scanned the room one last time before leaving. The fedora. Scooping it up from the sofa, he gently placed it back onto the bedpost.

The snow that had hit the Alps the day before had spared Munich, but the sky looked like it could change its mind at any time.

He started to leave, but saw his ski bibs on the sofa. The note from his landlord! He grabbed the note and shoved it into his front pocket, locked up, and headed to the train stop.

On the train he finally remembered the note. He pulled the crumpled white paper from his pocket and started to read. It said, "Karl, your mother called. It is urgent that you call her. Immediately, she said." It was signed with a wildly stroked S for Herr Schleichen, his landlord. Karl studied the note carefully and then crumpled it and stuffed it back into his pocket. His mother. What in the hell did she want now? Everything was urgent to her.

He got off the train on Maximilianstrasse near the Residenz, a few blocks from the Hofbrauhaus. It was ten minutes before noon. He knew the meeting was about to start. All of the meetings were on time. German efficiency. To the point. Short.

The large conference room, which was actually a cafeteria for employees of the headquarters, those who were not on the road, was nearly full. There was scurrilous banter and plumes of cigarette smoke coming from the corner where the seasoned drivers were gathered. Fritz was one of them. He winked and nodded at Karl, reminding him of his obligation to buy a few beers today. Karl smiled with confirmation.

The director of Bavarian Tours leaned against the wall smoking the last of a cigarette, his hand on the shoulder of a fine looking blonde, his secretary.

To the right of the room the tour guides sat rather quietly. Karl scanned those tables for a possible seat and especially for Angelique Flaubert. Then he noticed a hand waving for him. It was Todd Stewart, the Brit. Karl headed toward him and sat in a chair he had saved.

Todd wore black cotton slacks, a white shirt with black tie, and a never-ending grin. He was a slim man in his late twenties, a few years older than Karl. His face had appealing features, strong jaw, sparkling blue eyes, and a subdued nose, but his skin had been pock marked slightly from a bout of adolescent acne. It wasn't an overwhelming distraction, but more of an aberration of perfection. It was something Todd himself regarded as rotten luck.

"I see you've slept well again, Karl," Todd said sarcastically. His voice was proper and soothing, yet not unlike some character in a Monty Python sketch.

"Yes. You know the drill."

Todd nodded. "Up a bit late writing again? What are you working on this time?" He enjoyed hearing about Karl's newest story. Literature had been an important part of his life during his Cambridge days, until he dropped out of college to pursue his painting. Now, every spare moment was spent in front of a canvas or dreaming of his next subject.

Karl shifted his head toward the front of the room. The meeting was about to start. The director had extinguished his cigarette. "Tell you later over a beer?" Karl whispered.

Todd agreed with a flick of his chin.

The meeting was really inconsequential. The strengths of the company. Shifting of the seasons from winter ski tours to the spring line of tourist attractions. The company would be expanding to France, though. Those who spoke French would get a trip to Paris to learn all the highlights. That appealed to Karl. And his French would get by. It would mean one less time he would have to go into his spiel about mad King Ludwig and the three castles he commissioned to have built.

Throughout the meeting, though, Karl kept his eye out for Angelique. But she wasn't there, he was certain.

When the meeting ended, Fritz left the drivers and met Karl and Todd just outside the building. The midday traffic along Maximilianstrasse was heavy and loud. The three of them walked a few blocks to the Hofbrauhaus. It was Fritz's idea. His girlfriend was working, and he could fondle her buttocks without getting slapped.

In the Hofbrauhaus they sat on benches at the end of a long wooden table. The lunch crowd was there trying to keep up with the per capita beer consumption figures. The Bavarians were afraid the Czechs would jump into the lead. They couldn't have that.

After a few minutes, a Fraulein in a blue flowered dress, her generous bosom overflowing the low cut front, stopped by with her eyes on Fritz. She was a bit overwhelming for Karl's taste, but a postcard for old Bavaria. Fritz, his hand discreetly up her dress and planted on her left cheek, ordered three large beers. With a pretentious smile, she wiggled away from his paw and was off.

Karl paid for the beer when it came. "To Bavaria," Karl said, raising his glass. They clanged the large glasses together and then took long swigs.

"So, Karl, how was your tour?" Todd asked.

"Same obnoxious bastards who think they can ski until you get them on the gondola in St. Anton and they don't want to get off. Scared shitless."

"Not Billy Kidd, then?"

"No. More like Billy Crystal."

Fritz looked for his girlfriend. A brass band started playing typical tourist standards. When he noticed his girlfriend talking a little too long to another man, Fritz rose from the hard bench. "I must get rid of some beer. Wait 'till I return to order another."

Todd Stewart leaned over the table closer to Karl. "What about Batman?" Todd asked.

"I don't know. I still say it's a moral dilemma."

Todd shook his head after taking a long gulp of beer. "It's completely economic."

"Sure, economics are involved. But Bruce Wayne is clearly haunted by his own past. Morally he must conquer evil."

"That's just a front. I think he wants to keep making money so he can have all those cool gadgets.

The criminals represent the antithesis of righteous economic wealth."

"Maybe it's just the cool suit and babes."

Todd thought for a moment. "I'll buy that. What about Spiderman?"

"Don't get me started. He breaks all the laws of physics. There's no way those webs would hold him."

"Americans are so gullible."

"Right. Judge Dredd. Need I say more?"

The two of them gazed off at nothing and drank their beer. Karl couldn't help wondering what had happened to Angelique. Why she hadn't gone to the meeting.

"I have over a week off before my next tour," Todd said.

"Rub it in. That's the city tour?"

"Absolutely."

All the tour guides wanted that one, especially after the long winter season. Skiing was great, but too much of anything that could kill you was still too much. The city tour included Munich, Salzburg, Vienna, Innsbruck and Zurich. If the guide did even a marginal job entertaining the people, the tips would flow freely.

"How many buses?" Karl asked.

"Two. Mostly Americans and British. I've got one bus and Angelique has the other."

Karl fought hard to contain his envy. "What will you do with the time?"

Todd shrugged. "Paint, probably. Nothing too interesting."

Todd had studied art at King's College, practiced

fervently since his early youth in a wealthy family, and furthered his training at the university in Munich. Todd had befriended Angelique at the art institute and the two of them had become tour guides at the same time after answering an advertisement. It was the perfect job for artists. They usually had plenty of time off between tours, allowing them to paint and draw, and in Karl's case, write. And they traveled to many different European cities, where they could experience new museums and observe what contemporary artists were doing in those countries. Also, they could see the paintings by masters right in front of them, whereas others could simply view them in a text book.

Karl had just two days before his next tour. It was a trip to the Dolomites. Pain shot through his right knee just thinking of those sheer Italian slopes. His knee would never be ready in just two days. He thought about asking Todd to switch tours with him, but Todd wasn't an expert skier. It wasn't really a requirement, but Bavarian liked the guides to actually participate. It lent credibility.

They had one more beer before departing. Fritz stayed behind, his hand slid up his girlfriend's dress again.

Todd gave Karl a ride to his apartment in his little Fiat. Todd lived to the west of the English Gardens. He said it was merely a coincidence that he lived so close to the gardens, and not some Freudian attachment he needed to his homeland. Regardless, he did spend a lot of time there.

At the curb Karl asked, "Would you like to come up for a cup of tea?"

"Thanks, but no. I'm in the middle of a project that I can't seem to get off my mind." Todd was as compelled by his art as Karl was with his writing.

"Can we at least meet for dinner tonight at the Steinhaus?"

"Sure. At eight?"

"At eight." Karl gave the car door a quick slam and the Fiat sputtered away in a cloud of exhaust.

Karl got to the front door and noticed another note inside. The landlord again. There were never notes for the older couple on the second floor, only him. The landlord, who lived on the first floor, could always find them at home. He, on the other hand, was almost never there except to sleep and write. He flipped the note open. It was much like the first. Phone home. Urgent.

Upstairs he slumped into the sofa and put his hand on the phone. Finally, he punched in the long number to his mother's house.

"Schwaaaarz."

Karl had always hated the way his mother answered the phone. It was too perky. "What's up, mom?"

"I've been trying to reach you for two days." She paused for a moment. "I'm sorry, Karl. It's your uncle, Jack. He died two days ago."

A rush streaked through Karl's body. Uncle Jack, dead? "How!"

She paused longer.

"How?" he asked again. The anguish was obvious in his voice. He had no intention of hiding it. His chest heaved quickly. He knew he had to let it all out without stopping. Never had he felt like this. Never had he allowed himself to feel this way. But now he had no choice. He could no sooner stop this pain, than stop time from passing. And time had nearly stood still.

"He had been getting sicker and sicker," she started. "Cancer. He couldn't handle the pain any longer. When he could no longer teach, that was it. His mind was still there, and that was the hardest part. That brilliant mind. It was a waste, son."

Karl fought back tears. "Did he do it himself?"

She hesitated. "Yes."

"How?"

"I don't want to go into that."

"Quit trying to sanitize death!" Karl yelled. "How'd he do it?"

"A shotgun in the mouth," she fired back. "There. Are you satisfied?"

Karl sighed heavily. It was almost a relief. Uncle Jack would have liked that, he thought. Dying just like Hemingway. Dignity.

"We didn't set the funeral until we knew for sure if you could make it," his mother said. "Will you be there?"

Karl sunk deeper into the sofa. "I'll find a way."

CHAPTER 4

THE CRASH

After he got off the phone with his mother, Karl looked around his small apartment and the walls seemed to close in on him. He needed to get out. He started to leave when he glanced back and saw the sun shining in through the window, pointing directly at the fedora on the bedpost, with dust dancing around the outer brim like magical, mystical particles casting a spell on it. He smiled at the absurdity of his thoughts, but decided to bring the fedora with him nonetheless. He set the hat on the back of his head, locked up and headed outside.

It was a beautiful, crisp afternoon. The air was fresh. He could smell pastries from the bakery a few buildings away. He crossed the street between two cars and found an open bench in the park, where he sat back to take in the scene.

There were two young boys kicking a soccer ball back and forth. A mother in her thirties wiping the crumbs from a cookie from her young daughter's mouth. Two old men from the Great War sat on another bench, lying about old times, Karl guessed. He smiled, knowing they all seemed to be enjoying life, while he was thinking about the fragility of the human body. After all, people died every day to make room on Earth for those just born. There had to be some meaning to his uncle's death, yet he found his mind drifting off again, forgetting that he had just lost someone dear to him, and feeling guilty for having done so.

Karl thought about how he had first learned to love Munich. He had told the story to friends in Minnesota and they had stared at him dumbfounded. But then he told his friends Todd and Angelique the same story, and they understood completely, for they too had followed similar paths.

•

The three of them had finished eating dinner, and they were on their third or fourth beer—it was hard to know after a few good Bavarian beers.

Angelique had asked him how he decided to move to Munich.

Karl took a long chug of beer and said, "Did I tell you about the stay in the Innsbruck hospital."

They both shook their heads no.

Karl looked deep into his beer stein. "I never expected to be in Innsbruck," he started. "At least not at that point in my racing career. My coaches couldn't believe it either. I had worked my way up the World Cup standings. I don't know how." Some had called him possessed, but he knew it was simply determination.

"When I got to Axamer Lizum, I worked my way down the side of the mountain, studying each red and blue gate, each drop in terrain." He envisioned the scene in his mind. The bright light glistened off the snow and ice, blinding him from the truth, blinding his sensibility.

He continued, "I had to find the best possible line for the smoothest run. I knew that winners shaved a quarter of a second off each difficult gate, and maybe more off the easier ones. And in the end, winners won by less than a second. Yet, as in life, everyone makes mistakes. The key was to minimize the severity, conquer the mountain before it destroyed me. Nothing else mattered.

"The giant slalom wasn't my best event. As you know I preferred the quicker turns of the slalom. And this course was icier than I had ever seen. Just to stand on the side of the mountain without sliding sideways, was a great accomplishment. But then I thought of the ice as simply another impediment to perfection, something as inevitable as the rising and setting sun. I'd use the ice to my advantage. Learning to ski in northern Minnesota, where icy conditions prevailed, I believed that God had placed the ice there especially for me. I gained strength from it."

Karl took another sip of beer.

"So what happened?" Todd asked.

Angelique covered her eyes with her hand. "Is this going to have a happy ending?"

Todd laughed. "Do any of his stories?"

Karl sat up, determined. "Somehow, be it divine intervention or some celestial or subterranean force that I neither understood nor cared to comprehend, I was near the top of the standings for the first time since entering international competition. Less than a second off the lead. A good final run would give me a top three finish, possibly first.

"I was back at the top of the mountain, waiting my turn, squinting through those amber goggles I like. The wind whistled across the open valley from the northwest, and I imagined that that same air had been circulating since time began, breathed in by other great skiers, other great explorers or conquerors of unseen dangers. I took in a deep breath, closed my eyes and tried to summon the strength of greatness to inspire perfection. I let the air out and then inched closer to the starting house."

"He's not going to let this be happy," Angelique said. "La, la, la, la, la. I'm sorry. Go on. Ruin the night."

Karl continued. "A nervous Swiss skier stood before the timing gate, clicked his skis together one last time to clear invisible snow from the tops, propped his poles over the tiny gate, and waited for the countdown. Three, two, one. . . . He flew out of the crude little wooden shack and skated his way to the first gate." Karl swished his open palms together in a grand gesture. "In a few seconds the skier was over the first ridge and out of sight."

Todd and Angelique were on the edge of their seats. "Go on," Todd said.

"I closed my eyes and ran through the course with the other skier, tipping my head and body with each turn," Karl said, doing the same thing now. "In my mind, I cut the timing light with the Swiss skier. I knew exactly where I needed to be at each split time, each gate on the course. I was ready." He took another sip of beer.

"No wonder," Todd said. "He closed his eyes."

Karl ignored him. "I inched closer and stepped carefully into the starting house."

•

Karl leaned back in the park bench remembering what ran through his mind at that precise moment, when all that should have been there was the race. He had just won the state ski meet in the slalom and giant slalom, came home with the ribbons still slung around his neck, and pulled them out to show his mother. She simply glanced at the medals for a second and then said, "You missed dinner again, Karl. But I saved you some. It's in the refrigerator. You'll have to microwave it." He had thought of walking out the front door into the cold of winter, but he had nowhere to go. He went to his bedroom and threw his skis to the floor on the other side of his bed. Sitting down on the bed, he looked at himself in the mirror, where tears had formed in both eyes. It was then that he knew he could only depend on one person. Himself. She could no sooner acknowledge his success than realize she was no longer the high school homecoming queen. To recognize that he had achieved something, somehow diminished herself, vanquished her own existence.

•

He smiled when his mind flicked back to the bar with Todd and Angelique.

"Karl. Are you all right?" Angelique asked.

Karl shook his head. "Where was I? Oh, yeah. There was this official in a thick red down jacket. He ran his finger to the bottom of his clipboard, scribbled a check next to my name, and then smiled. 'Schwarz! Are you German or Austrian?' he asked.

"I considered the question. Did he mean now, or at some time? Bavarian," I said. He nodded and said, 'Good luck, Karl Schwarz, Bavarian.'

"I moved forward to the next man, the timer, who sat behind a small metal folding table. He was an older man who wore a headset over a black wool cap and spoke to another man at the finish line. 'Alles klar' the old guy said. He nodded his head toward the bottom of the mountain, and I took that as a sign to move to the gate. The countdown was a blur, as was the first part of the course. I knew at the time I was fast, faster than my first run, faster than anyone else that day. But it was at the peak of the speed for that course that would shroud my mind with total obscurity. It's strange to think back on the event. How I should remember preparing for the most important race of my life, and how I should forget about what really happened until reviewing the tapes nearly three months later. The mind can only understand that which is normal, earthly. Anything else is an aberration." Karl felt pain in his right knee just thinking about the crash.

"I knew this was going to get ugly," she said. "What about Monet?"

"What happened then?" Todd asked. "If you don't want to talk about it, that's fine we can discuss French impressionists."

Karl shrugged. "I don't mind." He hesitated for a moment and took a drink. "Once I saw it later, I remembered the icy turn that took my legs out from under me. There was this time in the air that seemed to linger and linger until I first hit my shoulder and head against the hard icy mounds, cracking my helmet and bones. There was darkness and the flapping sound, as if my brain were bouncing back and forth within my skull. I didn't hear the helmet crack, the poles bend against my ribs. Then darkness turned to brightness again, and I imagined angels slowly drifting down from heaven to the side of the mountain lifting me from a crumpled heap and raising my soul from my battered remains."

"Is this going to get worse?" Angelique asked. "All right, then. Renior? Anyone for Renior?"

Karl continued, "But the worst of it came as I flipped over to my right leg; it jammed into the hard-packed snow at an awkward angle and snapped like a dead twig."

Angelique cringed and shook when he said that. "That had to hurt," she said. "All right, damn it. How about Degas?"

"There was pain for only a moment," Karl said. "Then darkness. Darkness that would certainly never end. When I woke in Saint Peter's Hospital in Innsbruck, I lay in near-total darkness. I saw a few tiny red and green lights to my side, and I realized that somehow I had failed to be taken. Failed at my dream."

"That was you?" Todd said. "I remember seeing the crash over and over and over on the telly, thinking the poor sap must be dead."

Angelique reached across the table and held Karl's hand.

Karl started again. "I dozed off again and didn't wake until sometime later during the day. Now there was brightness. White tile floors, white ceiling tiles, white stucco walls, and even white marble window sills that seemed to suck in an iridescent light from the snow on the mountains off to the south. My right leg was hanging in some strange contraption of pulleys and cables. I felt my head. It was bandaged. I tried to sit up, but was forced back by the pain in my chest. The broken ribs.

"Over the next few days, all I could manage to do was think. I questioned in my mind whether I had simply dreamed that I had once been a great skier, had crashed and nearly gone to heaven, or if I was going crazy and had had some unfortunate auto accident. On the third day I was moved to a room down the corridor, which had, under normal circumstances, a splendid view of the mountains to the southwest. But looming there before me, much like a gravestone to a passing motorist following the death of a loved one, was Axamer Lizum, the mountain that had shattered my leg and shattered my hope with it. I couldn't bear to look at it. Not yet. So I had the nurses draw the shades until darkness, and then they would open them and I would gaze up to the bright stars, becoming as nocturnal as Galileo must have been. I found solace in the night.

"I talked with my coaches, who assured me I'd have a spot on the team the next year. But of course I'd need to work hard and earn my spot. Then the team left for another mountain to conquer, another race on the road to the Olympics. I knew they were lying. I'd be too old for the next Olympics. My chance had passed and I'd only have scars for memories."

•

Karl remembered thinking there, drinking beer

with his friends, how he should have at least been remembered. But he wasn't. Out of some strange reciprocity agreement by the International Olympic Committee, he would remain at the Innsbruck hospital for a month, fully covered by the Austrian government. He protested at first, but then realized that his stay in Austria, far from any questioning and consoling influences, was actually a stroke of good fortune. He would be forced to deal through introspection with whatever came his way, and that was the control he needed. Mistakes were far more severe having come from without than within. But he was isolated from anything and everyone he had known.

•

He gazed at his two silent friends and then continued, "That's where I learned German," Karl said. "In the hospital. My nurses and doctors spoke little English, so I was forced to learn German. I was told later that the doctors had feared they would lose me when I was first brought in, my pressure being extremely low, and they would hold me there until I recovered fully. They had no intention of bringing down international scrutiny on their fine city."

Karl thought about how the first call from his mother came almost a week after the accident. She had apologized for waiting so long, indicating she hadn't wanted to bother him and had only learned of the "fall" a few days ago. Karl said it was all right, knowing he was lying, and wondering how he would have handled it if he were the parent. She did give his room number to Uncle Jack, who in turn called once a week and sent him a box full of books.

The novels kept him going for the next few weeks. He had always been a great reader, having read most of the classics prior to entering college, and continuing for two years at the University of Colorado as an English major.

"My Uncle Jack sent me a wide selection of Hemingway, Faulkner, Fitzgerald and Joyce. I had read most of the books at least once, but I devoured them this time as if their meaning meant more than anything in the world. I wanted to be transformed back to Paris, sitting along the Champs Elysees drinking a beer and discussing works in progress, and dream of the future when others would envy the lost generation. It was at this time when I first scribbled a few notes of ideas I had for short stories and a novel. I envisioned myself plucking away in obscurity, working some inane job for food, and buying time for real passion."

"Well that dream sure as hell came true," Todd said with a laugh.

"I guess so." Karl stared across at Angelique, who still had her hand on his. "It was also there in the darkened room, with only a dim light to read by, that I started to understand Kafka. Perhaps I couldn't know despair until I had reached the damp bottom of the cask, or felt the pain of death lurking about. I too had become Gregor Samsa. And I too would redefine who I really was, or who I was meant to be." Karl finished his beer and ordered another one for each of them.

He remembered watching the Olympics from his hospital room in Innsbruck. One of the nurses rolled an old television into his room, and he watched the

Austrian and German coverage. There was no talk of him, really. One of the sportscasters mentioned him once, but it was more like a mocking of failure than anything. The isolation became even greater. When he could finally walk with crutches, he gained a little more inner strength, more confidence to occasionally gaze out his window and objectively forgive the mountain.

When the beer arrived at their table, Angelique proposed a toast. "To dreamers." They clanged their glasses together. "So, Karl. How did you end up in Munich?" she asked.

Karl thought for a second. "Well, a short while after I was discharged from the hospital I decided to take the long way home. I was still limping like crazy. One of my coaches had sent me a plane ticket from Innsbruck to Duluth with stops at Frankfurt, New York, and Minneapolis. I cashed it in for a non-stop from Frankfurt to Minneapolis, with two hundred bucks left over.

"I took a day train from Innsbruck to Munich, stayed in an off-the-wall Gasthaus for a couple nights, drank beer until the bars closed and walked the city streets for a couple more nights, like a young, desperate Aqualung.

"That's when I first fell in love with Munich," Karl said. "It's a large city, but you can't tell from looking at it. The autobahns skirt around the outer edge in wide rings, as if some magnetic force wouldn't allow them into the old town region. I liked that." Karl took another swig of beer. "I figured only those people who really wanted to be here, or had to be here, were here. All the other assholes just buzzed by.

"I would look at myself in shop windows near the Marienplatz and see a man who was lost but could be found. You know what I mean?"

They both nodded.

"A man beaten and downtrodden, yet with a small glimmer of hope set in the corners of my smile. I had forgotten how to smile. I also forgot my English for those few days, and with my jeans and wool coat I could have been just another German from some small Bavarian village. I felt at home." Karl took another drink of beer.

He continued. "When my money nearly ran out, I hitched a ride with a truck driver as far as Heidelberg. I spent the day at the university, and the night on a bench overlooking the Neckar, the moon shining brightly off the river. In the morning, I had just enough money to buy a train ticket to Frankfurt International.

"The time from the hospital to the airport seemed to linger and stand still. I don't know if you know what I mean. But it was a major turning point in my life. Have you ever had a time in your life when a short period determined exactly where you wanted to go, what you wanted to do with your life?"

Todd nodded. Karl had already heard the story of how he had found his way to Germany, after a falling out with his aunts.

Angelique turned her eyes down. She knew that her parents still had their hands in her affairs, and she didn't like it one bit.

Karl started again. "I had traveled to many places on the ski team, but those places were merely backdrops, valleys, to scenes that I never really saw. And now, for the first time, I could see the fluid motion of my past. Life beyond a dream that passed by in minutes. I could feel my heart beating, feel my mind clicking, feel, once again, that life had meaning."

•

Stretching back on the park bench, Karl pulled the fedora lower over his eyes, as if he were about to doze off, and then crossed his arms and legs. A large brown squirrel came hopping up to him looking for a handout, and when he had nothing to give it, it scurried away toward the two old men.

He couldn't help thinking about the part of the story he hadn't told his friends.

When he got home, his mother and father hadn't questioned what had taken him so long. They assumed he had taken a flight to his apartment in Colorado, the one he shared with two other ski team members. But after the Olympics, Karl had called his roommates and had them ship his stuff to an old friend in his home town. In fact, he had spent only that first night in Minnesota with his parents.

Karl gazed off across the park, wondering if he would end up like his uncle, a lost soul destined to blow his brains out. He had read of the sad and lonely life that most writers endure. Did the solitude have to lead to self destruction?

He got up and walked back to his apartment in a state of confusion, like a zombie without anyone to kill.

Inside his apartment he collapsed onto the sofa. He removed the fedora, propped his hand inside it, and studied the brown felt as if it had some magical qualities. He thought of the time since Angelique bought it for him at the Czech flea market. How his writing had improved. How his output had increased to a point he would have never imagined. Was it that inanimate piece of felt and leather and nylon ribbon? Was it really Franz Kafka's fedora? Did it matter? It's what he believed that mattered. And he already knew how Angelique felt about the fedora. She believed in fate and other mysteries of life.

He smiled, set the fedora back on his head, and leaned back on the sofa—dozing off almost immediately.

CHAPTER 5

THE STONE HOUSE

The third and final bell clanged in the twin towers high above the Baroque Theatinerkirche a few blocks down from Karl's place, waking him from his nap on the sofa. He slowly rose, drew back the lace curtains on the window, and gazed down at the street below.

It was overcast and seemed dark already. Light shimmered off the cobblestone boulevard as cars drove by, a brilliant luster, like a lighthouse beacon.

How had he found himself here and now? Were the couple walking on the sidewalk below aware of him, or were their minds blank to anything but motivation? Finding the right steps on the slippery walk.

After he had gone to the bathroom, Karl pulled a large bottle of beer from the refrigerator, popped the top, and poured the entire contents into a glass mug. The foam rose. Uncle Jack had said the foam was important. A good beer produced a thick foam and then stuck to the side of the glass as it receded. Now, Karl realized, he had tasted more fine beers than his uncle.

The foam had gone down far enough for him to

drink now. He raised his mug in the air. "To Uncle Jack. May you finally have peace in the midnight hour. Your wandering and wondering was why we understood each other."

He brought the mug to his mouth and took a long gulp. Then he sat on the sofa and flipped the cover up on his laptop computer. He realized that a part of his strength to persevere was gone. That was one way to look at it. But not the way Uncle Jack would have viewed his own death. He would have felt that the power that made him what he was, the strength that carried him through each day, had been passed on to Karl. Now Karl would have the strength of two men. Two dreamers. Dusk was always followed by dawn, he would say. And nothing was brighter than a new day. Strange how his uncle could say one thing and then live another, as if he didn't have the strength or courage to follow his own advice.

Karl took another gulp of beer. He looked at the computer and then slowly closed the top. He had to make it home this time. And he didn't have much time to prepare. He called the airlines and found a flight that would leave in the morning. Munich to Frankfurt. Frankfurt to Minneapolis, nonstop. And then Minneapolis to Duluth. He couldn't afford the flight, but he made round trip reservations and put it all on his Visa. He would return in six days. Then he realized he had a tour to Italy in two days. Maybe he could find someone to change with him. The obvious choice was Todd Stewart. He had almost a week off before his city tour. And Angelique Flaubert was on that tour as well. Todd's specialty fell more along the lines of apre ski, the night life. For many tourists that was even more important than the skiing.

He called the Bavarian Tours office and explained his problem. They would approve a swap if he could find someone to take him up on it. Otherwise he would have to take the tour or suffer the consequences.

He tried to call Todd, but there was no answer. He realized that when Todd painted he always silenced the ringer. Karl would have to go to Todd's apartment.

He slung on his leather coat, grabbed his car keys, and headed out the door. He rarely drove his old Volkswagen Golf. He never needed to drive, unless he went to one of the outlying towns, which were much easier to reach by auto. In Munich, the bus or train or his bike would take him anywhere he needed to go, and he was in walking distance of restaurants, bars and grocery stores. What more could he need? So the small green car normally sat behind the apartment building in a designated spot, collecting dust.

A light frosting of snow had fallen as he napped and settled on his car now. He disregarded that and merely cranked it over and let the front and rear wipers do the work for him.

Todd Stewart lived over a mile from Karl, two blocks off Kaulbachstrasse, between the University and the English Gardens. He had the best of both worlds, he would say. The University reminded him of Cambridge, although the similarity wasn't readily apparent, and he could stroll through the English Gardens on nice days to the Bavarian National Museum to gain perspective at the Schack Gallery.

After the short drive, Karl pulled over to the curb and parked. He noticed Todd's Fiat five or six cars up, and hoped that he hadn't wandered off somewhere. As he walked to the large brick building, he thought of how he wanted to approach Todd. He knew that Todd would do just about anything he asked, and the death of his closest uncle, whom he had mentioned numerous times in his company, was more than enough reason.

Karl hesitated on the steps and gazed up at the old building. Allied bombs had missed the structure completely, even though other buildings across the block had been destroyed and were now rebuilt from the rubble. Todd lived up one flight, and Angelique Flaubert held the apartment directly above his.

Karl went inside to the second floor. After pounding on the old wooden door and waiting, he looked up the staircase, wondering if Angelique was home. Todd finally answered. His expression changed quickly from annoyance to pleasure when he saw that it was Karl. Todd had changed from his more formal clothes that he wore to the meeting earlier in the day, and now wore light, tattered blue jeans with large holes in each knee. He had bare feet and chest and a long paintbrush in his left hand, the bristles still wet with a deep blood red. His sandy blonde hair lay in a messy heap, speckles of various colored paint here and there, as if he had grabbed his hair in a hasty gesture with the brush still in his hand.

"This is a surprise," Todd said, smiling boldly. "Come in. Come in." He whisked Karl in with his free arm and closed the door.

The apartment was much larger than Karl's. It was

long and narrow with windows overlooking the street out front and the University. In the back was the painting studio with a large window and a splendid view of the English Gardens. Karl walked directly back to see what Todd had been working on. It was not an obtrusive thing to do. They had a mutual respect for each others' work. Karl encouraged him as often as possible. He understood the sensibilities of an artist. The nurturing required.

Todd had found some success with his paintings. He had shown one piece at the State Gallery of Modern Art, had a small exclusive showing at an old town place, and had subsequently sold a few pieces for a meager profit. He was paying his dues, and that's the way Todd wanted it.

Karl gazed now at the large canvas. It was something that he had never seen before in Todd's work. A man lay naked in a pool of what appeared to be water. His eyes were closed and a light shone across his face. His arms, lashed with leather, lay precisely toward his soft penis. The lines were smooth, but there was a disturbing darkness about the entire painting. A surreal representation.

Todd came up behind Karl, placed his right hand on his shoulder. "What do you think, Karl? Be honest." He knew the request was more than anyone could handle. But Karl wasn't just anyone. Todd trusted him to be forthright.

"It reminds me of something I saw at the Louvre," Karl finally said, knowing it could be taken as nothing less than a compliment.

"Exactly!" Todd squeezed Karl's shoulder. "The Young Martyr by Paul Delaroche. Only that was a young woman with a classic halo over her head. This, of course, will be a red sea of blood as soon as I can get my shit together and make it work the way I want it to." He pointed now with the paintbrush in swirling strokes around the man's body.

Karl broke away and sat in a small wooden chair.

"But enough of me," Todd said. "What brings you by so soon? We were to do dinner tonight if my memory serves me."

Karl decided on the direct approach. "My Uncle Jack died. I have to go home for his funeral."

"My God, how?"

"He had been sick. Cancer. He couldn't take the pain any longer." Karl rubbed his pained eyes now, feeling the tears trying to escape again. Somehow he gained his composure. "I told you about him. I'm sure."

Todd came closer and put his hand on his shoulder again. "Yes. I remember." He wasn't sure how to react with Karl. He was never one to coddle the English stiff upper lip, nor had he ever been encouraged to do so. His mother and father died of some unknown disease when he was a child. His two aunts reared him the best they could, with his sentiment intact. He hadn't had to feel the anguish of the death of his aunts, but he could imagine the feeling as similar to what Karl felt now.

"I wouldn't ask this favor if for any other reason," Karl started. "But I have to make it home to Minnesota." He paused for a moment. "I have that tour to Cortina in just two days. I was hoping you could switch with me. I'd take the city tour when I get back."

"Of course. Without question." He looked up at his painting, which he would now have to finish upon his return. "I couldn't get that bastard right anyway." He threw down the paintbrush.

"But what about the skiing? Are you sure you want to do it?"

Todd spread his bare arms out wide in a grand gesture. "You know Cortina. I'll stick to the easy runs. Even those look spectacular with the sheer cliffs. Besides, I have a feeling that's where most of the tour will end up. And I know a few good bars to hit in the evenings."

Karl breathed a sigh of relief. He knew there was a touch of apprehension for Todd, and now he would feel compelled to reciprocate the favor in the future. And he would do at least that without question.

"What about dinner?" Todd asked.

Karl checked his watch. It was nearly four. "We could meet at eight as planned. We'll need to call the office and tell them about the swap. I need to get a few things in order before I leave."

"When is your flight?"

"In the morning."

"I'll drive you."

"Thanks. I'd appreciate that." Karl hesitated. "Do you think the dead really care if you go to the funeral?"

"Hell, no! But those alive do. You're going."

"I guess I should. It just seems so absurd flying halfway around the world for a one-hour service."

"It's been three years," Todd reminded him.

Three years! Had it been that long?

They said good-bye and agreed again to meet for

dinner. Karl got into his car and just sat for a minute. He wanted to see Angelique Flaubert before leaving. Needed to see her. Maybe he would call her in a few hours and see what she would be doing for dinner. He shook his head and drove home.

•

Karl occupied the next few hours packing a bag and staring off into nowhere. He would take only a carry on garment bag and his computer. Any more baggage and his mother would get the idea that he was there to stay, and nothing could have been more incorrect than that. He called the Bavarian Tours office to complete the swap. As he sat and waited for the late afternoon to fade into evening, he anticipated his return to Munich more than his trip to Minnesota. He hated funerals. He reasoned that funerals were invented for those who treated the deceased poorly while they lived and needed the time to repent their sins publicly as if they had been the best of friends. Only the dead knew the truth. He was sure of that.

The bells from the church rang out six times. He thought back to the first time he had heard the bells echoing against his building the day he took this apartment in Munich.

•

To some the Theatinerkirche was a cold dark structure, dank and dreary even on a sunny day. Yet Karl gained a certain warmth from sitting down on the hard wooden pews, gazing up at the Baroque dome, and wondering how many confessions had been heard there. How many times had someone come to this forgiving God asking for exoneration?

He had been told that you could never be cleansed of sin unless you confessed your wrongs. But why would those misgivings have to be verbalized? God should have known what he was thinking, without having him kneel before a mere celibate entity, a messenger of His will, and speak out on those things that some higher chaste man or group of men had deemed sinful over the years. Life was full of inconsistencies and irreconcilable pains that had made little sense. Why had God given him powerful lust at such a young age, if He didn't want him to act on it? It was a cruel joke. It was a sin to masturbate. It was a sin to have sex out of wedlock. Yet, the time between discovery of one and the realization of the other, was far too great for any man or woman to endure. So Karl knew that the forgiving God would understand if he held back with some of his sins. He could say his Hail Mary's and Our Fathers based on frivolous acts of lust, and not on actual action.

•

When it was within an hour of the time he was to meet Todd Stewart for dinner, he anxiously threw a sweater over his T-shirt and put on his leather coat. Without a thought to the contrary, he topped off his ensemble with the fedora.

It was extremely dark outside. Clouds had lowered over the city and light snow fell softly to the boulevard. Lamp posts shone as fading spots in the distance, and only came into view with each step he took.

The Steinhaus Restaurant was four blocks from Karl's apartment. It occupied the first floor of a large stone building. At one time the building had been a brewery, with its water supply from the nearby Isar River. But now the top four floors were converted to apartments for students and artists. Somehow the structure had also been missed by Allied bombings during the Second World War.

Karl entered through the wooden, castle-like door and stood for a moment looking for a table. Inside, the stone walls reminded him of the caves beneath the Liechtenstein Castle. Lights hung at the end of long metal poles from the high, dark ceiling, as if Neanderthal man had found a way to poke holes in his cave for skylights.

He was early. He took a table with four chairs, explaining to the Fraulein that he was expecting a friend. He was a frequent customer, so she knew without asking to bring him a large beer.

After a few minutes Todd showed up, dressed much as he had at the meeting earlier. He was fairly religious about his thin ties. He said it was merely a reflection of his youth. He had no intention of allowing it to be an indicator of superiority. He just felt naked in public without one.

They shook hands briefly and Todd took a seat next to Karl. "Just get here?" Todd asked.

Karl took a sip of beer and sat his mug on the table. "This long," he said, pointing to the half-full beer.

They both ordered traditional Bavarian meals, pork with a heavy sauce and potatoes and vegetables, and Todd got a beer as well. Todd seemed a bit off, though. Almost depressed. Karl realized that their emotions should be switched. But he wasn't sure why. They ate their meals without talking much, and then ordered another beer after the plates were taken away and Todd felt more like talking.

"You really like Angelique, don't you?" Todd asked.

"I think it's beyond that, Todd." Karl swirled his beer around the inside of his glass and took a long gulp. Then he added, "It's an impossible situation, really. I have no idea how she feels, but it doesn't really matter. In a few months she goes back to Brussels to marry someone she could really give a shit about. It's pitiful."

"You know she doesn't love him," Todd explained. He and Angelique had worked together for almost two years. They talked often. She seemed to feel comfortable talking with him. Karl knew this and often picked his brain for information on her. Todd would comply with all but those things she specifically declared off limits, such as her true feelings for Karl. She didn't want to give him any false hope, and that had been the hardest thing for her to hide.

"Whether she does or not is irrelevant," Karl said. "People marry for all the wrong reasons. Money, lust, obligation. When there are money problems, the marriage fails. When the lust has subsided, there is no longer a reason for the union. And when one finally realizes that obligation leads to subjugation, then too the marriage fails. But by then it's too late. People don't marry for love. It's too conventional. You know that."

Todd agreed with a nod. "There are exceptions, I'm sure."

"True. But what is love, really? Friendship personified? I have no idea how she feels about me." That wasn't entirely true, for one generally knows if another person is attracted to him. And Angelique had shown all those signs. She would linger with her kisses as they met each time, she would hold his hand as they walked, and her eyes. Her eyes gave away everything with her. If she didn't like someone, she would simply fail to maintain any eye contact whatsoever. With Karl, her eyes rarely wandered, other than standard sensual glances.

"Do you remember the Smurfs?" Karl asked.

"Is this some strange metaphorical transition? Freud would have found this contradistinction puzzling."

"Do you suppose they're androgynous?"

"No, no, no," Todd said, waving his hand about. "I think some huge ass snake shit them out and they hatched from eggs."

"But there's only one Smurfette."

"It's a bloody fluke of nature."

Suddenly, Angelique stepped up to their table. "What's a fluke of nature?" she asked.

Karl gazed up at her. She had a deep concern in her eyes that he hadn't seen before in her. He rose and kissed her warmly on both cheeks, and she the same to him, holding her cheek against his as if to gain warmth from the cold she had just left outside. She sat across from Karl and he returned to his seat.

"The Smurfs," Karl said. "Todd says they hatch from the eggs of a huge snake. I say they're like worms. Androgynous."

"The Smurfs are French, no?" she said, setting her jacket on the back of her chair. "That must have something to do with it."

Karl's eyes remained fixed on hers. "You're right. It's more likely they're tri-sexual."

"Tri-sexual?" Todd said.

"Right. They'll try anything."

"Sounds more like me," Todd said, as he rose and pushed his chair into the table. "I've got to get back to my painting and prepare for my wonderful Italian ski vacation. I'll see you in the morning, Karl. Don't keep him up too late, Angelique. He has an early flight to the States in the morning."

Before Karl or Angelique could respond, Todd was off and out the door.

After Todd was gone, Angelique and Karl gazed across the table like lovers having just spent the night together. She put her hand on his.

CHAPTER 6

FOUNDATION

Angelique ordered a glass of white wine, and when it came, she sipped it slowly as she watched Karl over the top of the glass. She twirled a strand of hair around her finger. She wore little make up and needed none at all. Her lips were flush with blood, and she licked them now to clear away a spot of wine.

Karl liked the way she moistened her lips, as if she were a model and the camera needed a highlight. He wanted to press his lips against hers and hold her close to his body. But it was impossible. He knew it and there was nothing he could do to change that fact. The more he tried to get closer, the further she would recede. It was always like that; had been like that almost from the moment they met. She would accept him as though there could be something between them, and then hastily back away, frightened by the prospect. It was as if she knew it was wrong to build a relationship, but the attraction was beyond any sensible power she had to control herself until, through some retrospective strength, or guilt, or some other hallowed force, she would prudently see her err in judgment. Karl allowed himself to close in, even with the knowledge that it wouldn't last.

She gave him a serious look. “I'm sorry to hear about your uncle.”

He peered at her lips as each word escaped. “Todd?”

She nodded. “He thought I should know.”

“I would have gotten a hold of you before I left for the States,” he said. “I have to go.”

“Yes, you must. I know what your uncle meant to you.” She took another sip of wine. “When do you return?”

“Just before the city tour,” Karl said. “Todd told you we switched, didn't he?”

She looked surprised. “No. That will be fun. I haven't been on that one for over a year. Have you done it?”

“No, I haven't. In fact I'll have to bring some materials with me on the flight so I sound somewhat intelligent.”

“That's never been a problem for you,” she said, and then smiled brightly.

They sat for a moment looking at each other. Anyone observing them now could mistake them for nothing but lovers. And yet they weren't. It wasn't for a lack of desire by either of them. She had her sense of responsibility, and he respected her for that. In fact, it was an endearing quality that attracted him to her. He only hoped that her convictions would somehow transfer from her fiancé in Brussels to him.

She wanted to change from the proper daughter

her parents always knew she was, to the independent woman with an ardent desire for someone she knew would never be her husband. She fought the urge every waking hour, and in her dreams. Somehow she would have to find the strength.

"My parents want me to come home for a long weekend," Angelique said. Her monotone meant she was reluctant to leave.

"Are you going?"

She shrugged. "I don't know. Adrien will be there," she said without sentiment.

"And?"

"And he wants to make plans for June. Late June." She looked at Karl as if she wanted help. If he could only force her to stay in Munich. Force her to not marry Adrien. He could do it with only a word, 'stay.'

"Tell him to piss off. You don't love him. Why are you going to marry him?"

She sat quietly. She wanted to agree with him. Admit she was wrong. Admit she was stupid for going through with the marriage. But somehow she couldn't allow the words to pass her lips. She could only say, "I must. My parents . . ." She stopped to formulate the words, as if she had practiced them from a script, trying desperately to understand them herself. "My parents depend on me to do the right thing."

The right thing, he thought. How in the hell was getting married to the wrong man, a man she had no feelings for whatsoever, constitute doing the right thing? He swished his head back and forth slightly and then took a long gulp of beer, finishing it. "I'm sorry, Angelique, but that's bullshit. I don't see that as the right thing. A guy cuts his ear off for a woman and then can't figure out why she doesn't love him. I'll tell you why. Because the freak only has one ear."

"It was a wonderful professing of his love for her."

"No! He needed to give her time. Maybe paint her a nice picture of flowers."

She laughed aloud. "It's all I've got," she muttered.

"You can have anything you want, Angelique. You're a beautiful woman that any man would be happy to have. Never sell yourself short. You have so much going for you. You have a job that you love. You're a wonderful artist. You have friends that adore you. And at least one who more than adores you." He smiled at her now.

She reached across the table and placed her soft hand on his. "I wish things were different. I want to do the right thing."

He grasped her hand. He wanted her without complications, but he would have her even with them. "Do what your heart tells you. Your heart will never fail you. You believe in fate. Follow that."

Tears formed in her eyes. "I don't know if I'm strong enough for that. My family is so powerful."

That was a recurring theme that Karl had heard for months. But for the first time she said the words with less power. Less persuasion. He had never seen her quite like this. It was as if she wanted him to make the decision for her. Normally, she was the one with the strength to say that her marriage was an inevitability not worthy of discussion. Stop the conversation with one determined glance. It was refreshing to see this side of her. Yet, he still didn't understand the change in her.

She was certain that he noticed a loss of dominance in her. But she no longer cared. He was a friend like she had never had. They could talk for hours about everything and nothing. It didn't matter. He could talk for hours about a story he was writing, or the novel in progress. She would sit, content with each utterance, as if what he was saying was the most important thing in the world. In a way it was to both of them. They would visit art galleries and she would discuss her art, content with the knowledge that he was truly interested. He would listen for hours to her constant recitation about her duty to her family. He would listen, but not understand. And she too wondered if she understood. She wiped the tears from her eyes and finished the glass of wine.

"What are you thinking?" he asked.

She looked up from her wine glass. "I'm confused. I don't know what I think. Would you walk me home?"

"Sure."

Outside, more than two inches of new snow had fallen softly to the ground. There was a certain freshness in the air, as if the snow falling through the atmosphere had cleaned it, cleansed it of all impurities. Traffic was light, slowly sneaking up the lane, their headlights like parallel moons drifting across the sky.

Karl wrapped his arm around her shoulder and they walked slowly down the boulevard. Neither said a word for a few blocks.

Finally, she said, "I'm going to miss you, Karl."

He stopped and looked at her. Large snow flakes speckled her hair. But it was her serious expression that caught him off guard. "It's not like I'm leaving forever."

"Maybe not, but I have this strange feeling you're not coming back. Or if you do, things won't be the same. There will come a time when we have to say good-bye forever. I don't understand my feelings, I just have them." She slung her arm around his waist and pulled him to walk again.

In a few blocks they reached the outside of Angelique's apartment building, stopping at the base of the high brick steps. On the second floor, Todd Stewart's light was on.

She couldn't feel the cold from the snow, the bite from the wind against her face. She only felt the warmth of Karl's smile, his reassuring arm around her shoulder. Looking at him now, his plaintive smile and his long lashes fighting off the falling snowflakes, she could have just pulled him upstairs to her room and made love to him through the night. And the thought had occurred to her. Pulled at her now. If he would only ask to come in, there would be no way she could refuse him. Or want to.

He was so comfortable with her. By any measure they should be together. He felt now more than ever there was something special between them. Nothing contrived. But something that was even more inevitable than her marriage to a man she didn't love. He believed, perhaps more so than anything tangible or without abstraction, in his inner feelings. And those positive feelings for her were astronomical in proportion to anything he had felt in the past. Anything.

He wasn't aware of the time. It could have been midnight or four in the morning. He had an early flight. Had to leave. But if she would ask him up to her room, he would do so without question. He envisioned the two of them in her room, slowly undressing until each was completely naked, each savoring every aspect of the other's body with eyes and tongues and hands, until they finally embraced and joined and made love until dawn. If she would only ask.

They stood in the cold warmth of the evening snow, still gazing at one another. Finally, when it seemed as though they had been frozen in time, she moved closer, tugged on his leather collar pulling him to her, and kissed him passionately on the lips. It was a kiss that would linger in his mind for eternity. Their first true kiss on the lips. So natural, yet so unexpected for both of them. They slowly drew back a few inches.

"You have to get up early," she said softly, her breath freezing in a cloud toward him. "I look forward to your return . . . and our city tour."

"I have a feeling it will be the best tour I've ever been on." He smiled and then wiped a little speck of snow from her nose. "Will you be going to Brussels this weekend?"

"I don't know." She was pretty sure she did know, but was still not sure if she had the strength to endure what would come of her decision.

"I guess I should be going," he said. "I have an early flight."

She nodded. “I’ll see you when you get back.”

He watched her climb the stairs, unlock the door, and then go inside. He stood there for a moment, wondering if he should follow her and pound on her door, but decided against it. Up on the third floor her light flicked on. He watched and waited for a moment longer, hoping she would open the window and call down to him. Ask him up to her apartment. Her silhouette appeared for a moment at the window. She was pressing her face against the glass, looking for him. She set her right palm against the window and held it there. Karl waved, turned and shuffled down the slippery cobbled sidewalk toward his home.

When Karl got home, he shook the dampness out of his leather coat and the fedora and then in a chill he hadn’t felt all evening, cranked open the radiator valve to allow it to pump out more heat. He put the fedora on the bed post and then sat on the sofa and checked his watch. It was a few minutes before midnight.

Somehow he could feel the fedora calling him, so he turned his eyes toward his bed. Kafka’s fedora hung over the bed post as if it contained the mind of the man himself, urging Karl to put it on and gain the wisdom that only time and failure and retrying could bring in one man’s lifetime. It was almost as if he had acquired some hidden truth. Some hedge on life that others would have to nearly die for, yet he had found erudition in the simplicity of felt and leather and a nylon ribbon. If guilt had ever found a home in languid truth, then Karl had become a sluggish, burdened man. And he didn’t care.

Hurrying to his bed, he slipped his hand inside the fedora, quickly set it on his head, and returned to the sofa.

He turned on his computer, called up a story he was working on, and his mind went blank. He fiddled with the fedora and then stared imperceptibly at the gray screen. He had no intention, really, of adding to the story this night, but he had conditioned himself to at least make the effort. That's what he would keep telling himself.

When he knew for sure he had no desire to write, he turned off the computer and checked the bag he had packed earlier; clothes for four days. He could wash them if he needed to. The idea was to appear in Minnesota with nearly nothing, so his return was inevitable. After he was done, he flung the bag to the floor.

He stood and paced back and forth a few times in the small room. Now he was torn over what to do. In just six hours Todd Stewart would knock on his door to drive him to the airport. In eight hours his plane would take off. And now his thoughts were mixed over whether he should even go. Would it matter to Uncle Jack if he showed? Do the dead know the difference? After all, he needed to go not to please those who remained, but to see his uncle one more time. To try to reach the understanding they had reached so many times, especially the year and a half he had returned to northern Minnesota. Would it matter, though?

And would Angelique feel the same when he returned? Karl was sure there was something special between them now. Something that could be lost forever if he got on that plane in a few hours. She could go to Brussels and her parents and Adrien would convince her she was doing the right thing by marrying him in June. She knew she didn't love him, and Karl was certain she had strong feelings for him. Yet, there couldn't be appreciation without deprivation.

He sat on the small bed in the corner, set his alarm for five, and then lay down slowly. Looking around his small apartment, he realized that the only things that belonged to him were the bike, the skis, the computer, and various other insignificant items of everyday life. Uncle Jack had always said that people are only renters on this Earth. Even a house isn't really owned. Someone pays the mortgage for thirty years, which is actually just rent, and then they die and the relatives sell the house so the vicious cycle can repeat itself. He had always said things like that with a sly grin, as if he knew something special and had just passed the information on to him.

Then Karl noticed the picture on the nightstand. It was the only picture he had of Angelique. Todd had taken a shot of her and Karl on skis high on a mountain overlooking Innsbruck. It was a trip they had taken in December, on the company, to kick off the ski season, much the same as the Zugspitze trip where he had first met Angelique. Bavarian Tours called it a training session, but that had to be the greatest misnomer in history.

Karl undressed and clicked off the lamp. In the darkness he thought again about his night with Angelique Flaubert. Like so many other nights, he thought of them together. All he had was his dreams.

In the morning he would be sure to find an answer to his doubts on staying or going. The dawn always emerged with insight.

•

He woke to a pounding on his door.

"Karl, it's Todd," the muffled voice said after the last volley of knocks.

He made his way to the door in his underwear and opened it quickly. Todd Stewart looked him over for a moment and then came in and closed the door.

"What the hell were you dreaming about?" He had a small white bag in his left hand. And then the distinct smell of croissants filled the air.

Karl checked his watch. It was a few minutes to six. His alarm must have failed.

"Are we going?" Todd asked.

Karl saw his packed bag next to the door. He rubbed his hand through his hair. "Yeah, I guess."

In a few minutes of scurrying about the room throwing last minute items into his bag, Karl was ready and they headed out the door. At the last second he grabbed the picture of Angelique from the back of the nightstand and slid it into his carry on bag and clutched his computer under his arm. He stopped one last time at the door, gazing back at the fedora on the bedpost. Something tugged at him, forcing him toward the fedora. Without a choice, he put on the fedora and left.

They both ate a croissant on the way to the airport. Neither said much. After Karl picked up his boarding pass at the ticket counter, they stood for a moment just outside the security area for international departures.

Todd shook Karl's hand. "Have a good flight."

"That's not up to me," Karl said, smiling.

Todd started to move away and then stopped.

"What's the matter?" Karl asked.

He struggled with the words and finally said, "Nothing. I guess I'll see you after you return."

"After the city tour," Karl corrected. The tours overlapped with the city tour returning four days after the Dolomite ski trip.

"Right."

They shook hands again and Karl headed through the security area.

CHAPTER 7

PERSISTENCE

Karl had been on the plane for over two hours trying to settle in to the constant drone of the engines and the movement of people up and down the aisles to the bathrooms. He had a window seat, his eyes were closed, but he couldn't sleep. His mind kept drifting back to Munich.

•

It was near the end of his job with the publisher in Munich when Karl first met Angelique Flaubert. He had been spending more and more time on the weekends at the university library researching the life and works of great authors in the English section. He felt he needed to know how other writers had lived their lives, coped with the dangers of solitude and insecurity and rejection, to fully immerse himself into his fiction. After all, if one couldn't personify the image or perception of a writer, then half the fun would be lost in the not doing.

Karl first saw her in early October, almost a year and a half ago. He remembered distinctly, because he had gone out the night before to an Oktoberfest celebration, had far too much beer, and sat that

Saturday in a rather subdued state staring at Kafka's Metamorphosis as if it were a children's fairy tale.

She strolled by the first time as if she were one of the Eumenides discreetly seeking him to punish him for an unknown sin. Her beautiful auburn hair flowed over her shoulders and bounced with each step. Her eyes seemed to shift in his direction. She looked like a typical college student. Blue jeans that hung over her hips as if they were borrowed from her father. A baggy sweat shirt with sleeves pushed up to the elbows. And comfortable leather shoes. Nothing restricting. He imagined, even then, that she was hiding a splendid body under all those clothes.

When she passed by again, selected a book from the shelf as if she had been looking precisely for that selection all her life, she glanced his way and smiled briefly. It was barely a turning up of the lips, but Karl could tell that she had a nice, warm smile. He wanted to see more.

As quickly as she had appeared, she was gone. He made a note of the exact time he had seen her. People were creatures of habit. If she came that Saturday afternoon, then maybe she would the next, he remembered thinking.

He couldn't get the vision of her out of his mind all week. At work all he could see was the flash of auburn and the half-smile. He was distracted with everything and couldn't do his job—a job that had become more and more difficult each day anyway. If he had to translate another boring text book, he was certain he would slit his wrists.

As Saturday rolled around, his mind became more

focused on the auburn girl. He didn't know her name yet, so that is what he called her. He thought about his last time at the library. He had been hung over and probably looked like hell. This time he made an effort to look his best. He wore his finest jeans, a white shirt, and he actually combed his hair.

After selecting a biography of Fitzgerald, something he had already read once, he took a seat and waited. Karl always sat at an old wooden table with four chairs in an isolated spot. He liked the privacy. With four chairs and only one person at the table, it wasn't likely that someone else would sit down.

It wasn't long before the auburn girl made an appearance. Just as she had before, she slipped by quietly the first time and then stopped on her second pass. This time she smiled fully. A rush streaked through Karl as he returned her smile.

The encounters continued for eight weeks in a row. She even came closer on a few occasions. Karl was going crazy. It had become a game with no end in sight, like chess between equal opponents. Work had become intolerable, and his writing had changed. Changed for the better, as far as he was concerned. Something about her had inspired him to write with a conviction he had never been able to understand in all that he had read about other writers.

Karl's life changed profoundly in December of that year. He had met Todd Stewart in the library right after an encounter with the auburn girl. After talking for a while, Todd realized they had a great deal in common. So he asked Karl to go skiing at the Zugspitze the following Saturday. Todd had explained that he wasn't a great skier, but he enjoyed Garmisch so much that he tolerated the cold slopes as an excuse to retreat to a fireplaced bar. Karl, thinking about his weekly encounters with the un-named auburn girl and not wanting those to end, decided to take him up on the offer nonetheless.

It was a decision that Karl would later thank Todd for repeatedly. Karl didn't realize until he got to Garmisch that Todd was there with a group from work; Bavarian Tours. Todd had only started with the company a few months before, and the entire group of tour guides were there for a seminar to teach them how to handle large groups of American and British tourists.

Just before noon, while waiting in line for the tram, a women shuffled up behind Todd and Karl. She wore a hat and goggles. Then she flipped her goggles to her head and said hello to Todd. Karl didn't recognize her at first, since he had never seen her without her hair flowing over her shoulders and without jeans and a sweat shirt. Todd introduced her as Angelique Flaubert, one of the other tour guides. The three of them skied the rest of the day together, and when the day was done and they had discussed their job with him, Karl knew what he wanted to do. With Angelique and Todd's prompting, Karl met the boss and showed how he could ski and speak German.

The following Monday, Karl gave the publisher notice and immediately went into training as a tour guide. At the time he had no idea what was required of the job, but that didn't matter. For, deep down, he really wanted to be closer to Angelique. The fact that he would meet hundreds of interesting characters, which would be extremely beneficial to him as a writer, was secondary.

A year passed. Karl learned his job well. His ability to converse with people from all walks of life made him an extraordinary host. His salary increased with favorable comments received, and his tips were generally greater than what others received, although there was a great deal of under reporting on the part of some. He was making as much as he had working for the publisher, but without all the angst. He enjoyed the work, and his writing became even better than he suspected it could. He had even starting sending short stories to small magazines with some success. He also started the novel. Part of his success, he knew, was due to his ability to bounce ideas off of Angelique and Todd. Their relationship, that of Todd and Angelique and Karl, was built on mutual trust and an understanding of each person's desire and passion for a dream that others couldn't comprehend.

Karl spent the year constantly seeking Angelique. He had to be near her, if for no other reason than proximity. After a few months Karl learned that Angelique was to marry a man in Brussels. It slowed him down, but didn't break his resolve.

She showed no real conviction when she talked about her fiancé, so Karl's friendship with her continued to strengthen. They discussed every possible subject. They would eat together, drink late into the night, and do coffee early in the morning.

He remembered a few months back, when he and Angelique had met at the bakery less than a block from his house. He was wearing the fedora she had bought him. She liked the way it looked on him. He looked like a writer, she thought.

He set the fedora on the table against the window after kissing her and sitting down. They drank coffee and ate strudel with ice cream.

"I love this place," Karl told her. "I found this bakery the first week I returned to Munich."

She sipped her coffee, peering over the top at him. "You never told me why you came back here," she said.

"It's a long story," he said.

"I have time." She smiled at him and touched his hand.

"All right. I told you about my skiing accident and my first real visit to Munich prior to heading back to Minnesota."

"Yes. We got so drunk that night."

"I'll say. Anyway, a little over a year after the skiing accident I graduated from Northern Minnesota University. It was May. I had nearly tripled my course load for three quarters to finish in just over three years, including the two at Colorado. I had lived and breathed writing and reading for a year and a half. I didn't really give a shit about my other classes, although some of them were interesting and helpful for me as a writer. I took German also to keep honing my skills.

"In June I packed my backpack with enough clothes for two weeks, the new laptop computer my Uncle Jack gave me for graduation, and bought a ticket for Frankfurt. I shipped my old ten speed touring bike in baggage, and would ride throughout

Europe for the summer. That was the plan anyway."

"What happened?" she asked.

"My Uncle Jack saw me off at the airport, wanting more than anything to have the courage to go along with me. When I reached Germany, I loaded my bike and started heading south along the lonely red roads that linked tiny villages. I spent some time in Heidelberg, perfecting my German. I'd camp in farmer's fields or on groomed forest floors or in nature parks. I ate mostly bread and drank water and beer, yet I seemed healthier than at any other time in my life. Even my knee felt fine. Sure there were occasional bouts of pain in the evening following a long day's ride, but nothing like the anguish of atrophy from weeks of inactivity living in the college library.

"I followed the Neckar to Heilbronn and then veered east to Schwabisch-Hall, Aalen, picked up the Danube to Ingolstadt, and finally headed south to Munich. It took a week to get from Frankfurt to Munich, but I was in no great hurry. Getting there was less important than how I got there."

He paused for a sip of coffee. "One day along the Neckar, I stopped for a drink of water. While I cooled myself off, I watched an old man tending a hilly section of Reisling grapes. His tools were crude, having more rust than polished metal, yet he took the time to smile as he wiped the sweat from his brow. Then the old man walked down the hill a ways to me, leaned against his rake, and pondered me for a moment.

"Finally the man asked in a slurred German dialect, which I still remember distinctly, 'Why do you ride on such a hot day?'

"I thought for a moment and then said, 'The faster I ride the cooler I get.'

"The old man smiled. 'Yes, but the faster you ride the less you see.'

He paused, staring at the fedora. "I thought of all the drivers in their Mercedes and BMWs and Porsches cruising along at two hundred kilometers per hour on the autobahns, pondered my own bicycle, and laughed. 'In a car I would have never seen you working your grapes,'" I said.

"Would that have been so bad?" the old man asked.

"I think so."

Karl finished his coffee and poured another glass from a small metal pot. Then he continued, "The old man had me up to his tiny tractor, produced two large beers and a sandwich from a cooler, and we ate and talked for over an hour. The man explained his small wine growing operation from start to finish, and I briefly detailed my dream to write. When I was off on the road again, I realized at that moment, more than any other time, what I had to do. I stored the man in my increasing pile of characters that would one day emerge to life again on the pages of short stories or a novel."

"Did you use him in that story about the old man who lived in the alpine village and hadn't been to the city in over fifty years?" she asked.

"Exactly," Karl said. "You know, I fell in love with Munich all over again the first day I arrived. I had admired the city on my trip following my recovery in the Innsbruck hospital, but now it was as if I could no longer pedal my bike for fear of breaking some enchanted spell. Most of my days over the next week were spent at the Marienplatz or the University. I took the small room I still have, intending to stay only a week.

"I'd take day trips riding into surrounding villages, testing the local beers. I wrote daily. I became a regular at this place. The owners, an older couple, allowed me to plug my laptop into the wall socket below this table. I didn't bother anybody, and I spent what little money I had on bread and beer while I wrote stories."

"How did you get on with the publisher?"

"Well, money had become a problem. After a month, I got serious about finding a job. The German government is very forgiving of foreigners working in their country, as you know. After a week of intense searching, I found the job as a translator with a small publisher."

"What did you do there?"

"I converted English and American text books for German secondary schools. It was my job to ensure the idioms and colloquialisms seeped through with a semblance of meaning in German. My writing was suffering though. I dealt with words and texts all day long, languishing in a tiny cubicle, with a boss whose management style was molded by Gestapo training flicks. I felt like Kafka must have, working for the insurance company. Yet, I needed the money, and needed the job to stay in the country. As you know, I lasted nearly two years."

•

Karl was shaken from his reverie by the man sitting next to him in the center seat. It was time to eat. A flight attendant handed him some food, and he looked at it as if it were a pile of dog turds. He wasn't hungry, that was for sure. He picked at the chicken a little, and then settled on a warm bun with some butter. After shoving the dish aside and closing his eyes again, he was finally able to sleep.

CHAPTER 8

HEILAND

Minnesota had a hundred towns like Heiland. Small towns of stoic Scandinavians and Germans lured from the old country to cut down the forests and mine the iron ore and build their dairy farms. They found the woods similar, built homes, built lives and endured the frozen tundra and the wolves killing their cows.

Karl's grandfather had come to the northland and found work logging. His father had moved indoors and worked since seventeen in the Heiland paper mill.

His mother, Maxine Schwarz, on the other hand, was born into a family that owned a clothing store in Duluth.

Now, Maxine poured a cup of coffee and sat at the kitchen table. She gazed out the back window, where snow swirled in tiny tornadoes on top of the crusted, frozen surface, and the sun barely peeked through the clouds and the naked trees. She wondered if Karl would come home. Maxine's hair hadn't been combed yet, and the brown and gray massive mess, which was normally pulled up to the back of her head, lay tangled across her slumped shoulders. She wore an oversized flowered kimono that hid the imperfections of her flaccid body. Nonetheless, she had big bones. Exercise had never meant a great deal to her, for she believed that God protected those with good hearts, regardless of temptations and flirtatious overindulgence.

Maxine glanced at her sister, and picked up her stare.

"I guess I'll have to get my own, then," Claudia said, as she rose from her chair and poured herself a cup of coffee.

Claudia was two years younger than her sister and had more gray and less wrinkles. From the neck up, the two could never be mistaken for anything but sisters. Yet, Claudia was in far better shape physically than Maxine. She loved to walk the little roads of Heiland, if for no other reason than to be seen and to see. There was always something more interesting going on than at her empty house. Her skunk-like streaks of gray hair, as she often reminded people, came only days after the first time she was struck by lightning.

"I'm sorry," Maxine said. "My head isn't straight, ya know. Too much has happened in the past few days. I was wondering. . ." She stopped short. Her sister needed no more fuel to ridicule. Claudia was capable of picking up any insignificant detraction and turning it into something it wasn't.

Claudia sat at the table across from her sister. She understood her sister's anxiety perfectly, and it was an opportunity for her to exploit.

"Oh, I'm sure he'll come home this time," Claudia

said. She could easily dismiss the situation. After all, Jack's death meant nothing to her. She never liked him anyway. He was always too confident for her taste. And she felt no remorse whatsoever speaking ill of the dead. Life wasn't like the movies, where the corpses rose from the grave and tormented the living. Not in any truly physical way, anyhow. At least she hoped not.

"I'm sure he'll come home," Maxine said. "Dad's death was one thing. He'd been near death all Karl's life. It was almost a blessing."

"Yeah, fur sure he'll come," Claudia assured her. She sipped her coffee slowly.

"It's different this time. Jack meant so much to him. He was like a father . . ." She held back and sipped her coffee.

"I don't know why he lives in that foreign country anyway," Claudia said. Her nose wrinkled as if she had smelled something repulsive. "Alla his relatives there are dead, am I right? Killed during the war. He coulda just said he needed ta find himself like everyone else, ya know. But he had to spout off some nonsense that made no sense to me. And it's been three years now without even coming home for Christmas. If I was his mother, I'd demand his presence." She slurped her coffee, her eyes drifting up over her glasses for a reaction.

The phone rang, startling both of them.

Maxine stared at the ringing phone, thinking she should have taken it off the hook. She had done nothing but answer the phone for the last two days, listening to hesitant callers hedge the issue of suicide. It was as if she had had some control over the situation. She who had talked with Jack only infrequently at family weddings and funerals in the past five years, and only slightly more often than her husband. She knew the callers meant well, but couldn't help feeling that they merely thought there was a disease in the family. An ailment that God would never forgive, and Jack would surely float endlessly in Purgatory for his sin. What other explanation could there be? The callers, friends whose friendship would change forever because of the act of one person, had mostly meant well. However misguided their sympathy, they at least had made the effort to comfort her in her time of need. That had to be worth a few points when their time came.

When the phone stopped ringing, tears formed in Maxine's eyes. She didn't want to cry anymore. Jack had been more what she expected out of a man, even more than the man she no longer slept with. It had been so long ago that they were close, yet they had never reconciled. She could never forgive herself for that. The thought she had wondered for twenty-six years haunted her still. Those memories would remain until she too died and was lifted from the world of sin.

"How'd Karl sound when ya talked with him?" Claudia asked.

Maxine shifted in her chair and sighed. "Not good."

"Is he coming home?"

Maxine nodded. "Fur sure." She noticed her sister's skeptical expression. "Ya still don't think he'll come? Jack was everything to him. He encouraged him to follow his dream to become a writer. He coulda just taken his English degree and become a teacher like everyone else, but that wasn't his goal."

"But what about a family?" Claudia pleaded. "He's almost twenty-six years old. He should be thinking about settling down. Starting a family. What was wrong with Dee? She's a beautiful girl, and she adored him. Still does, I'm sure."

Maxine wanted to reach across the table and smack her sister. She would have too, if she hadn't thought of how she would have been perceived. Claudia should have never brought up the family, having married and then failed to have children herself. And it wasn't for a lack of trying, according to her deceased husband, but because she, who talked of children often with great reverence, had been secretly taking the pill. Without even her husband knowing. She had had the audacity to force him to have his sperm checked for vitality. When that had backfired, she had said they failed to do it enough, or not at the right time, or he had been away too much. All lies, of course.

Maxine swished her head back and forth. "She's still a beautiful girl, ya know. And I hear she's not married yet. I saw her at the mall a few weeks ago, and she said she still gets postcards from Karl once in a while."

"He never sends any to me," Claudia said.

Staring at her in wonder, Maxine said, "Why don't ya color your hair?"

"God gave me this after the second time He struck me with lightning."

"You musta really done somethin' to get his goat like that."

"You can't just brush mine away with Hail Mary's."

"It was good enough when we was kids," Maxine reminded her. "You and that Parker boy down by the river. And on Sunday."

"Don't you go pious on me. By the way, are brothers about the same?"

Maxine leaped from her chair and sprinted toward the door, looked out into the dining room, and then turned back toward her sister.

"Don't ya ever say anything like that again!"

Claudia seemed to sink into her chair, but her point had been made.

CHAPTER 9

SIBLINGS

Down in the basement, Dan and Laura Schwarz sat at the bar. Dan was a few years older than Karl, and Laura was four years younger.

"Do ya have to do that so early in the morning?" Dan Schwarz asked his sister. He grabbed the bottle of whiskey from her hand and put it back behind the bar.

Laura gave him a critical glare. Her long blonde hair, which lay in a strange contortion about her face, hid a beauty that had once been, and could be again, the desire of any man. She wore a tight, black aerobics outfit, with a g-string that crept up into her butt crack with each movement. She pulled her heavy breasts, which had nearly fallen out of the skimpy suit, up by the straps of her top. She was in outstanding shape, despite abusing herself first with sex in high school, and later with alcohol. Youth had a tendency of forgiveness that wouldn't be so forth-right with age.

"You can stop the big brother shit anytime now, Danny. I'm twenty-two, ya know?"

It wasn't worth arguing and Dan knew it. But his

sense of responsibility stretched beyond mere age. She would always be the little sister he tried to protect. He walked over to the sliding glass door that allowed access to the basement for only four or five months of the year. Snow had drifted two feet up the glass, was drifting now with the gusting northeast wind.

"What a horseshit day for a funeral," he said.

"Wake," she corrected, and then pulled the whiskey from behind the bar again. "The funeral is tomorrow." She poured herself a shot glass to the top. "Ya gawk at the body at da wake and then ya say good things about the dead guy at the funeral."

"Whatever! It's still a horseshit day. Why in da hell do we live way up here?" He turned in time to see Laura suck down the shot of whiskey.

She coughed and shook her head. "What'd you say?"

"I said, why in da hell do we live way up here?"

"Because we're fucking idiots. We love to torture ourselves, basically."

"You betcha!"

He couldn't totally disagree with her. Even though he complained about the weather and other negative aspects of northern Minnesota, like the mosquitoes that could carry small dogs away, he would live in no other place. They both knew this.

He sat on a wooden stool at the bar and pulled the whiskey bottle closer. "Where's mom?"

"Up in the kitchen with Aunt Claudia."

"What else is new?" He poured himself just over half a shot and quickly flipped the contents down his throat. Warmth streaked through his body. He felt ill, near puking. When he had almost recovered, he said, "How in the hell do you do that?"

"Practice." She smiled and then her expression quickly turned to incertitude. "Why are you wearing that paisley shirt?"

Dan Schwarz looked down at his sleeves. The shirt was green and brown with large and small swirls, much like hippies wore in the late sixties, but clean and pressed.

"Paisley is perfect. You can wear it to work. You can wear it to the beach. You can wear it to the movies. You name it, you can wear paisley there. So why not a funeral? Besides, I went to the office this morning for about an hour. An appearance mostly. But I had some work to do."

She didn't understand his work completely. He had gone to the trade school in Duluth for electronics, but he worked at the paper mill in an office now. After their father got him a job there, he had worked on machinery. But regardless of how many times he tried to explain it to her, she was still baffled. What he did was really not that important to her as long as it was something without too much controversy.

She changed the subject. "Are ya sure mom said Karl was coming home?"

"Yes! For the tenth time. But you know Karl. He has a hard time with commitments."

"Not when it comes to Uncle Jack," she said. "He could do no wrong. What flight is Karl coming in on?"

"Hell if I know," Dan said. "He never said. But I guess we could call the airport."

She swished her head back and forth with great

exaggeration. “They wouldn’t give the information,” she said. “It’s against the law. Some kinda Privacy Act shit.”

“Are you serious?”

“Fur sure.”

He picked up the phone book at the end of the bar, found the number to Duluth International Airport, and called. After a few minutes of explaining his problem to an unimpressed operator, getting nowhere fast, he concluded that Laura was right. But at least he found out when the flights would arrive that day. He slammed the phone down. “What a buncha shit. Ya usta coulda do it.”

“I told ya. You shoulda trusted me, brother. I do work at the court house. When are the flights?”

“One at noon, one at four, and one at nine tonight,” Dan said. “All from Minneapolis. Knowing Karl, I’d guess the nine o’clock flight. I spose one of us’ll have to go get him.”

“Don’t sound so enthused.”

“Well God Dammit. What in the hell is he living in Germany for anyway?”

She shrugged. “I don’t know. He hasn’t been the same since his accident. I know it was tough on him not making it to the Olympics, ya know. But it’s like he’s torturing us for it. And he still skis all the time. That’s gotta be painful.”

“It’s stupid. He’s a bullheaded citiot now. He’d ski even if his broken bones poked from the skin. I can understand that passion, but I’m not sure about his writing. Does he really expect to make a living at it?”

She swished her head. “Now I understand the

writing. That's Uncle Jack. Karl's last year of college was dedicated to writing classes, some with Jack, and others with his cronies. Karl lived and breathed it. You didn't see it, 'cause you were off with Wanda every second of the day."

"Don't even mention that bitch's name," Dan scowled. Two years had passed since the divorce had been final. There had been no children involved, but that hadn't changed the complications of the procedure with public accusations of infidelity on both sides. He could have made a rude comment about Laura's failed marriage as well, but that was too recent to bring up.

"But he can't make a living as a writer," Dan said. "Even newspaper writers don't make diddly-squat."

"Mom said he's had some short stories published in magazines or something. But you're right, he didn't make much off that. Says he's workin' on a novel."

"Right," he sneered. "And I'm going to make a million bucks on da stock market." He paused for a moment looking into the bottle of whiskey and deciding at the last second not to have a second shot. "Is he still playing tour guide to a buncha obnoxious Americans?"

"Think so." She poured another shot for herself and after a slight hesitation gave him half a shot also. She raised her glass. "To Uncle Jack." She furled her thin eyebrows into a jagged point as if they were the tip of an arrow pointing down her narrow nose toward her brother's glass.

"To Jack," he said without conviction.

They both pounded the whiskey.

Dan shook his head violently. When he was done, he rubbed his finger behind his ear and then smelled it. "Smell this," he said to her, forcing his finger under her nose, which she promptly shoved aside.

"You're crude."

"What ya spose that is? You get it on your finger and it lasts all day."

"Try taking a shower," she said, and then got up and went to the old stereo next to the fireplace. She dug through a pile of tapes before settling on Sade. Then she turned it on and danced her way sensuously to the window, swaying her thin hips to the soft voice as she watched the snow churning outside.

Dan moved up behind her and planted a hand on her tight buttocks. "You've still got a nice ass for an old cheerleader," he said, squeezing a handful.

She furled her brows as she gazed at him over her shoulders, still swaying her hips. "How long has it been, Dan? You need to get laid."

"About as long as its been since your husband left with a new boyfriend?"

"Fuck you," she said, turning back toward the window.

CHAPTER 10

UNCLE JACK

Karl woke abruptly with the turbulence of the descent into Minneapolis/St. Paul International Airport. He looked around and the flight attendants were collecting empty cups and cans. He had only an hour layover before his flight to Duluth.

Once he landed he headed out onto the concourse and checked the gate for his flight. He was just a few gates away from his next flight, so he went into a bar, got a beer, and took a seat by the window. He gazed off at the frozen tarmac, wondering why people lived so far north in such extreme conditions. The pilot on the plane had said the temperature outside was twenty below, forty below with the wind chill. And the wind was howling out there now, swirling snow around the baggage carts.

He started thinking about his Uncle Jack, and how he said he only remained in Duluth because he had reached tenure. Only now did Karl realize that the safety of a job shouldn't dictate true desire.

•

He thought back to when he was in college, taking classes with his uncle and his colleagues.

When Karl had gotten back from Germany after his skiing accident, he immediately enrolled in spring classes at Northern Minnesota University. There weren't many classes to choose from, since it was so close to the beginning of the term, but that didn't matter. He would have taken anything at that point. Anything to take his mind off skiing. The long days in Innsbruck and the short stay in Munich had given him new strength and direction.

Luckily his Uncle Jack was an English professor, and allowed him into an upper division course in American Literature. It was those two and a half months from the middle of March until the end of May that sealed his relationship with his uncle.

Jack, reveling in his newfound freedom as a divorced man, would ask Karl to his house on weekend evenings to discuss literature and writing. There were other professors in attendance, but Karl was the only student. At first they seemed to be speaking a foreign language, with esoteric jargon that spews from the mouths of all English professors, but eventually he understood. He loved to argue the quality, or lack of quality, in the established American canon. His rakish comments were tolerated, almost revered, by the high percentage of women professors in attendance. They thought he was handsome. Karl could converse with the best of them and still find time and inclination to play with a few of them sexually during his time as a student. Most didn't want him in their classes for fear of slipping up, showing favoritism, and fearing that he would have nothing to do with them for some noble reason.

It was also during that short spring that he began

to form a basis in his life that would forever change how he thought of himself. He had always seen the world around him as a stage of props, waiting for the next actor to enter his life and somehow change his perception of reality. But now, he was an actor. Whereas dreams had been some obscure image of night or day with no discernible beginning or end, they were now focused on a result. Sure, he had dreamt of winning a gold medal, but that had been different. More of a plasticine image of himself standing on a platform as the national anthem droned in the background. Now he saw people as future characters in a fiction that hadn't been written.

The summer after his first quarter at the university, Karl took a canoe trip in the Boundary Waters Canoe Area Wilderness with Uncle Jack. Ten days of canoeing from lake to lake, portaging up to a mile across rocky hills and swamps, fighting off droves of mosquitoes, with moose and wolves and loons their only companions. Professor Jack Schwarz threw aside his tweed and became a fisherman; blue jeans, flannel shirts, and hiking boots the daily uniform.

On the third night of the canoe trip they were sitting before the campfire, a mild breeze out of the west kept the bugs at bay, and a red glow painted the clouds like an Italian fresco.

Jack looked at Karl, who was burning the end of a stick in the fire, and said, "If you could do anything you'd like with your life, what would you do?"

Before his accident and his stay in the Innsbruck hospital, Karl would have been able to answer that without even thinking. But now he pondered the question carefully. He lit a large cigar and puffed hard on it to keep it going. "A writer," he finally said.

Jack tried to smile. "I wanted that once." He threw a few more dead twigs on the flickering flames.

"What happened, Uncle Jack?"

"I got married," he laughed. After a moment of silence, he said, "Seriously? I tried to write, but I had nothing to say. I'd heard my professors telling me of similar debilitations ever since Freshmen Comp 101, and I'd thought of it as myth. After I got my first degree, I tried to write serious fiction. Something that would enshrine my soul in the being of mankind for eternity, or at least become a footnote on some grad students' papers. But I hadn't lived yet. I'd gone to school and never stopped to take in the world. One cannot write of the world without having taken part. So, what did I do?"

Karl took in a puff of smoke and shrugged.

"Went to grad school. Great fucking idea. Linger longer in the world of academia. The more and more I read of the established canon, writers on the fringe, and even obscure practitioners, the more I realized that I was deficient in my human education. Oh, I knew all the greats by then. Could quote with the best of them. But I still hadn't lived. How in the hell could I write about some man obsessed with a prostitute, if I'd never even seen one? Shit if I know. So I did the logical thing, went on for my doctorate. My God, what a waste of time. Don't you ever do that. I want you to promise me right now that you'll never go on for your PhD. Promise!"

Karl raised his right hand. "No problem. I promise."

"When you go on for your PhD, you lose any creativity that you've ever had. Why do you think Hemingway, Faulkner, or Fitzgerald never got a degree? They were too creative to even think they'd need it. Too arrogant as well, but that's beside the point. You can be arrogant if you can back yourself up with the written word. And they could. Well, I had a touch of creativity at one time, but it was squashed like a bug under the boot heels of all my professors. All they ever wanted was sources, sources, sources. And now I find myself asking for the same damn thing. I used to wonder: what ever happened to original thought? I couldn't even ask myself that question, let alone my professors. You see, they get you when you're young and vulnerable. Make you believe that you're nothing but some robot spewing out some critic's thoughts of some reviewer's assessment of some poor soul's writing that they may have languished over for a decade, written in their own blood. Who in the fuck are we to judge them? Any of those authors who have surely produced something more than us. At least they've tried."

Drawing back and taking a long puff on the cigar, Karl thought long and hard. He had never quite seen his uncle like this. Sure he had always been passionate, even reverent to some extent. But he had never heard Uncle Jack trash his own profession. "So, you took the path well traveled and it made all the difference?" Karl said.

"Exactly. I should have veered to the right and

gone off through the woods. Screw the path. This is life, Karl." He stood up like Moses about to part the Red Sea. "This is the world. If you want to write, experience life and people before you try to enshrine them for all humanity. I'm not saying to drop out of school, Karl. Finish your bachelor's and then move on. You could be done in a year and a half, but then get the hell out of Duluth, get the hell out of Minnesota, and experience life."

Karl and Uncle Jack had stayed up most of the night talking about life. Karl had thought at the time that he knew where he was going, but only needed a path to follow. And now Uncle Jack had said there was no favored trail. Somehow Karl knew this to be the truth. He always had.

•

"Excuse me, sir," came a voice.

Karl looked up at a waitress with big hair.

"Would you like another beer?" she asked.

He checked his watch. "No, thanks. I have a flight to catch."

She raised her brows, glaring at him strangely.

Then Karl realized he had answered her in German.

"I'm sorry," he said. "I have a flight."

She smiled at him. "Nice hat."

He had almost forgotten it was there. "It's a fedora," he said.

Shrugging, she pranced off.

He finished the last of his beer and headed toward the gate.

CHAPTER 11

DEE O'BRIEN

The sun was already near the horizon at the end of the runway when Karl's plane swooped down over a frozen Lake Superior and landed high over the hill in Duluth. The barren pines, frozen in time awaiting a spring that was still months away, reminded him more of a tundra than a place he had once called home.

After picking up his bag from the carousel on the lower level of the two-story terminal, he went to a pay phone and stared at it blankly. His brother and sister both lived in Heiland, but he had no intention of calling either of them. Nor would he even consider calling his parents. He knew his mother would be fussing over food. His family always ate well during weddings and funerals, and his father . . . .

Karl flipped through the pages of the phone book. Then he realized that all of his friends, the few that he had, had escaped the frozen north for warmer places. At least they thought that the Twin Cities were warmer.

The only real friend he had was a woman everyone expected him to marry, and he hadn't. But they had reached a mutual agreement where friendship was far superior to a forced relationship that they both would have probably regretted.

He found Dee O'Brien's number in the book. She still lived in the small house above the Big Schlamm River that her lawyer father had bought for her. He slowly punched in the number. He checked his watch and wondered if she would be home from work by four-thirty.

She answered on the fourth ring with a simple "Hello."

He hesitated for a second. "Hi, this is Karl."

"I heard you might be coming home," she said. Her voice had a certain quality to it like a soft-speaking D.J. on a late night classical station. She could have told him to fuck off right now and he would have stayed on the phone for a minute to savor her words. "I'm sorry to hear about your uncle."

He always felt uncomfortable in these situations. He wasn't sure whether to be grateful or gracious. He settled on, "Thanks, Dee." He thought for another moment. "Hey, listen, I'm in a bit of a jam. I'm at the airport and I could really use a ride to Heiland."

She didn't find this strange at all. She agreed without question to pick him up, and would be there in thirty minutes.

While he was waiting, he went upstairs to the bar for a cold beer. Three years had passed since he had seen his family, and he had no intention of doing so without at least a few beers.

When almost thirty minutes had passed he went back downstairs and waited by the loading ramp. If

Dee said she would be somewhere in thirty minutes, he could set his watch by it. Karl gazed out at the frozen parking lot below. There were few cars. The ramp was completely vacant. No taxis. Nothing. There were so few flights through Duluth, that the taxi drivers knew when each would arrive, and only came by for the infrequent fare.

In a few minutes a new Toyota Celica came up the half-moon ramp and stopped out in front of the arrival door. The cloud of steam pluming from the exhaust gave him the first real indication of just how cold it was outside. He zipped up his leather coat, realized it was useless to even attempt to keep the bitter cold out, went outside, threw his bag into the back seat, and got in the front, setting his computer on his lap.

She stared at him for a moment. She wasn't sure how to approach him anymore. She had tried to be forceful in the past and it had gotten her nowhere. She had tried subdued and he had ignored her, or at least, she realized now, forgotten about her. It had been almost four years since they had made love all night in her waterbed. She felt a twitch deep within herself at the thought. They had been great together, but the sex hadn't been enough to cement their relationship. He needed more. He never said so, but she could tell.

He realized that she hadn't changed much in three years. Her curly black hair was well below her shoulders, whereas it had always been right at her shoulders. That was a nice change. But at twenty-five she could have easily passed for twenty. She had a youthful, perky smile that she would most likely carry with her throughout life. She was beautiful and he knew it was just a matter of time before she would marry and change their relationship, whatever that currently was, forever. He finally said, "You look great." And he meant it.

"So do you, Karl." She smiled now and then realized that she was staring and started to drive away.

They headed back toward Heiland on slippery country roads. Darkness was nearly complete. They didn't talk for a while. Not far after they reached the interstate, Karl finally asked the question he had wondered about since she picked him up. "Are you seeing anyone?"

"Yeah," she said quickly, not looking at him. "I just ended a relationship with a guy. He was a manipulative, jealous type in his thirties, ya know. But he acted like a damn teenager. It was nothing serious as far as I'm concerned. What about you?"

He wasn't certain how to answer that. After all, Angelique was destined for marriage. He wanted more than anything for the answer to be yes. "No."

"Maybe we'll never marry, Karl." She glanced at him for a second now. The lights from the dash brought a strange green glow to her face. She meant never marry in general, but it could have been taken both ways.

"Maybe not," he agreed.

"What about sex?"

"What about it?" Karl asked.

"Are you at least staying in practice?" she said smiling.

"Not as much as any man would like. My hand gets a hell of a workout. But then I don't have much time for it either. Traveling all the time."

"How are the European women? I mean, do they shave yet?"

He knew what she meant. "Amazingly they have the same body parts as American women."

Talking about sex made her want him even more. She would do just about anything to feel as she had the last time they made love.

They exited at Heiland and she headed toward his old house. She glanced at her car clock. It was five-thirty. "The wake is tonight at seven," she said. "Johnson Funeral Home. Would you like to stop by my house. I could change and we could go there together, eh?"

She was wearing nice black slacks and pumps now. He had a feeling she wanted to do more than just change. "Sure. Do you have any beer?"

"Yeah, fur sure."

She drove straight to her house. It was a small house over fifty years old. Two bedrooms, one bath. It was larger than any one person needed, yet not quite big enough to escape from someone you wouldn't like to talk to. This wasn't the case with Karl and Dee, but Karl had imagined that over time the size could have been a problem. The edge of her yard, which was frozen with stacked, crystallized snow, sat high above the Big Schlamm River. On a good day the river was putrid. Bad days were far more common, with the paper mill upstream. The house sat far enough back from the river to be no problem in a flood. Besides, the river was dammed a half mile upstream and controlled by the power company. Karl could never remember a time when the river had even crested above the bank enough to dampen her yard. With the house and yard came five acres, mostly pines, cedars, willow and alder. She also had three large apple trees that would drop fruit for the deer.

As Karl walked toward the house, his knee nearly gave out, and he twisted it back into place. He continued on, limping badly.

"Is the weather bad for it?" Dee asked.

"Yeah. It doesn't help. Anything above twenty degrees isn't too bad. But twenty below? Forget it."

Inside, Karl noticed a number of changes since the last time he was there. Her entire kitchen was new. The carpeting had been replaced. Different furniture. He went to the refrigerator and pulled out a beer. There was a six pack of German beer, and he wondered if that was just a coincidence. He went into the living room and sat on the sofa.

Dee was already in her bedroom changing.

"I talked with your mother at the mall the other day," she yelled. "She looks good. Sorry to hear about Laura's divorce. She's takin' it kinda rough."

Karl shifted his eyes around the room, not sure what he was looking for.

"The weather really sucks, ya know," she said. "Then the summer comes and you can't go outside with all the mosquitoes and black flies. You hear about Jill Starky? Probably not. Anyway, she was killed in the Twin Cities last summer. Murdered. Some say she was a hooker. I wonder how she woulda explained that at our ten-year reunion? Anyway. . . ."

Dee came out wearing a tight black dress, black

high heels, and dark nylons. She flipped her hair over one shoulder and turned her back to him. "Could ya zip me?"

"Sure," he said, rising.

He zipped and fastened the dress at the top and she turned quickly to face him. Much of her cleavage was showing, so she slowly pulled the straps up and adjusted her breasts into some state of equilibrium with the dress.

He took a seat on the sofa again. She walked with a precise new sway into the kitchen and got a beer. On her way back she stopped for a second at a bulletin board next to the phone. She un-tacked five or six postcards and brought them with her. She took a seat uncomfortably close to Karl and crossed her nice legs, hiking her skirt even higher. She flipped through the cards slowly. He had sent them over the last couple years. There was Rome, London, Berlin. He stopped her when she reached one of Notre Dame Cathedral. It was a night shot taken of the back from the water side. The rampant arches stretched out like the ribs of a starving man. He remembered buying the card from a street vender in Paris on a personal trip he had taken almost a year ago.

"I guess I'll have to learn a little more about this pretty soon," he said. "It looks like our company will expand to France this year."

"You must really have to know a lot for your job."

"Only if you want to sound somewhat intelligent. We do study each place thoroughly. I have a hard time with some Americans. They think a fellow American couldn't possibly know as much about

Europe as a European. So I give them a little show sometimes. I use an English accent or a German accent and become someone else for a week."

"You're kidding, right?" She took nearly everything he said as the truth, but occasionally her fault became his laugh.

"No, I'm serious. I don't do it with the ski tours because once in a while someone remembers me." They didn't actually remember him, but more his name and how the American sports announcers had nearly blamed him for his accident, dashing the team's hope for a medal in the slalom.

"How's your leg?" She placed her hand on his right knee gently.

"It's not bad while I'm skiing. But from twelve to twenty-four hours afterwards it seems to fill up with fluid and there's a great deal of pressure and pain. I'm sure I'll need surgery again in five or six years, but by then who knows, I might have had my fill of skiing anyway."

"I doubt it." She knew he would ski until he died.

She looked at the next card, a panoramic view of Munich. He moved closer and pointed to a spot on the card. "That's where I live, more or less." It was an indistinguishable spot of brick buildings with red tops.

"How do ya like it there?"

He pondered his answer. "It's really nice. It's better for me than some other Americans since I speak the language."

"Do ya have friends?"

"Yes. I have two friends who are guides, a Brit and a Belgian woman. There are a few other American writers there. Rich kids mostly, trying to spend as much of their parents' money as humanly possible. I don't take them too seriously. They seem to have a high enough regard for themselves. A few have left recently for Prague. Munich has become passé. And of course, there's Fritz. He's a driver who I team up with most. A good Bavarian who likes his beer. The Bavarians are good people. A bit more personable than other Germans. Easier to get to know."

"What about your writing? How are things going?"

He knew this question was coming, would come from most of his family, but he hadn't quite figured out how to answer it from her. Of all the people in Heiland, other than his Uncle Jack, she understood him best.

He shifted on the sofa away from her a little and took a sip of beer. "It's coming along," he finally said.

"Your mom said you've had a few short stories published."

He nodded. "Yeah. Literary magazines. They don't pay shit, but then I don't expect much. I look at it more as training for my novel. Paying my dues. I'm about half way on that."

She gave him a look, as she always did when they discussed his writing, as if he were some stranger from the past explaining something that she should already know. She checked her watch. It was less than a half hour before they should leave for the wake. They decided to have one more beer before taking off.

Just when they were about to leave, there was a

knock at the front door. Dee looked through the window and shook her head.

"What's the matter?" Karl asked.

Dee held her hand on the door knob, not knowing what to do. "It's the guy I told ya about." She hesitated for a moment. "He's been bugging me. Calling me. Driving by. You know. A regular pain in the ass. It's why I dumped the bastard." She tried to smile.

"Have you called the cops?"

"Well. That's a problem. I'll get rid of him." She opened the door to her shoulder, keeping her foot propped against the bottom.

Karl watched her, but couldn't hear what they were saying at first. Then the voices started rising, and he saw her struggling with the door. He swiftly rose to help her, but by then the man was through the door and into the living room.

"Who da fuck is this?" the man yelled, pointing his finger at Karl.

"This is Karl," she said, in no mood for introductions. "I told ya he was coming home for his uncle's funeral."

The man considered this. He was about the same size as Karl, but he had a paunch. His hair was cut in a flat top and seemed to stick straight up like that of a pissed off dog. He had this dumb look on his face, with one eye that would wander uncontrollably. He fiddled with the zipper on his leather bomber jacket. "I thought you were just bullshitting me, Dee Dee."

"Dee Dee?" Karl asked.

"You shut da fuck up," the man said, poking his finger into Karl's chest.

Karl's blood started to boil. He didn't like to fight, but he wouldn't walk away from a jerk like this. "You want to save that finger, I'd remove it."

The man didn't budge.

Dee moved closer. "Bud, I asked you nicely to move. Do you want me to call one of your friends?"

"Go ahead. Dey know you're a bitch."

That did it. With one fluid motion, Karl pulled the man's arm toward him, putting him off balance. Then he swept his leg under the man's feet, flopping him to the carpet. Karl pounced on his chest and punched him quickly in the nose and mouth. There was instant blood.

"Ah, dammit," Dee said. She ran to the kitchen and returned with a wet towel, throwing it at the man.

"What da hell did ya do that for?" the man screamed, trying to get up.

Karl helped him to his feet and toward the door. The man was so preoccupied with the blood he didn't understand where Karl was leading him. He led the man to the sidewalk outside and squared up with him.

"When the lady tells you to leave," Karl said. "You better listen."

"Or what?" the man said. It sounded strange and muffled, since the towel was in front of his mouth and the blood clogged his nose.

Karl thought for a moment. "Or I'll kill your ass."

The man stared at him. Then he pointed right at Karl again. "That's your last mistake, buddy."

Karl felt Dee pulling at him. "Let's go, Karl. Get inside."

Reluctantly, Karl followed her in and closed the door behind him.

"What an asshole," Karl said.

Dee was sitting on the sofa, her hands covering her face.

"What's the problem?" he asked. "I was just kidding about killing him."

"Ya don't understand, Karl. He's a county cop." She stared up at him, tears streaking each cheek. "I've gotta live here. You don't. In a few days you'll hop a jet back to Germany, and I'll have ta put up with that asshole."

Karl sank into the sofa next to her, put his arm around her shoulder, and her head against his chest. "I'll take care of it. I'll call the sheriff."

"They're good friends," Dee sobbed. "He won't help."

"What about the county attorney?" Karl asked.

She nuzzled closer to him. "Maybe."

"Your dad's a lawyer. Doesn't he know a few judges. Hell they all golf together I'm sure."

"I didn't want to call in any favors from him," she said. "He told me not to date a cop from the beginning. Can we change the subject?" She checked her watch. "We better get going, ya know."

CHAPTER 12

THE WAKE

For Karl a wake ranked right up there with a root canal or being cornered in airports by religious zealots. But it was at least one place ahead of funerals. There were words spoken at funerals that brought back memories which were best left in the minds of individuals who really knew the person—not some preacher for hire with a congregation of hypocrites.

The Johnson Funeral Home resembled a fast food restaurant in a strip mall. The only difference was a lack of enticing aroma wafting from outside vents.

As Karl and Dee walked up the long red carpeted aisle, glances and murmurs followed them. Dee stopped to talk with Karl's mother and sister.

Karl stopped at the casket with stares piercing the back of his head. The first thing he noticed was the casket, a beautifully smooth red wood with swirling grain. Cherry, he guessed. The inside was a plush white silk. When he could no longer admire the fine workmanship, he forced his eyes toward Uncle Jack. His hair seemed more red than he remembered, like half-washed blood. His ponytail was pulled over his left shoulder. His gray red beard was trimmed to the point of near perfection. It had always been scraggly from constant pulling and combing with his fingers as he read or lectured his classes. His nose and cheeks were a flesh tone; makeup covered a natural rosy tint. He liked how they had dressed him in his favorite gray tweed jacket, a trademark of Jack's.

Trembling as he thought about all the conversations that would be lost now, Karl's knee nearly buckled beneath him.

Karl reached down and touched his uncle's hand. It was cold and the hairs on the back of his hand felt like bristles on the belly of a porcupine. The room seemed to press in on him. Echoes of muffled voices and laughter, smothering infectious laughter, deafening. He closed his eyes, and now he was lying looking up at people. How natural he looked. They do such a good job nowadays. How could he have done that to himself?

A hand rested gently on his shoulder. He opened his eyes and saw Dee next to him.

Nudging his head next to her, he whispered, "How the hell'd they do it?"

"Do what?"

"Fill in the hole in the back of his head."

"Karl!"

"I'm sure my mother forced them to do it," he said. "Denial isn't just a river in Africa. It's everything in Catholicism."

She looked at Uncle Jack more closely. "It is remarkable."

"He looks so . . . what? Like a damn wax figure at Ripley's?"

"Jesus."

"No, nothing like Jesus. Jack would find this totally surreal. Look at these people. You know what they're thinking?"

Dee shook her head.

"They're thinking, what now? Is there something more than this? More than flesh and bones?"

"Isn't that normal?"

"Nothing is normal."

He wrapped his arm around her waist and they slowly walked to a corner of the room and sat down.

After a short period, he noticed his mother shifting her eyes in his direction. He didn't want to talk to her yet, but then he realized that perhaps the timing was right. She would never make a scene in public. God would punish her. If God was that vengeful, Karl wanted nothing to do with Him.

His mother sat next to him, fumbling with her rosary. Dee got up and went across the room to talk with Karl's sister, Laura.

"You shoulda called and told me when your flight was," she whispered to him. "It's a good thing ya have Dee as a friend."

"I figured the family would be busy."

"I got your old room ready for you. You must be tired from the flight. Ya don't have to stay here very long."

"Dee said she'd give me a ride."

"Danny's there. He came by earlier. Some of the relatives from the Twin Cities will be coming by later." She got up. "We'll talk back at the house."

He nodded. That meant she would talk and he would attempt to listen. He watched the people, wondering what great insight he might derive from them. Lingering in small groups were some of Uncle Jack's fellow professors and former students. There was still no sign of Uncle Jack's ex-wife or his son, Geoffrey. Not that he really expected either of them. The divorce had been quite final. And Geoffrey was probably off on the planet Zenon.

Karl hadn't seen his father, either. He strolled over toward Laura and Dee. He had never seen his sister in such disarray. And it was her appearance that had always set her apart from her peers.

He kissed Laura on both cheeks. "Sorry I haven't written, sis," he said softly. "Writers are the worst at letters." In truth, he hadn't even called her when he found out she was getting a divorce. And now the divorce was final.

"That's all right," she said. Her voice wavered from alcohol, and the smell lingered in the air like death itself, laughing at the living. "Ya know how much I write."

He put his arm around Dee's waist. "Could we head over to my parent's place? Get a beer?"

Dee gave Laura a quick glance. "Fur sure."

Laura gave him a stupid grin. "I'm way ahead a ya, bro."

They walked down the aisle and out into the cold darkness. The sky was filled with stars. The air was always so fresh on nights like this, but as Karl took in a deep breath his nostrils collapsed and froze and he realized that it was nights like this that made him appreciate his new home.

It was only six blocks from the funeral home to his parent's house. When they got there, Karl pulled his bag from the back, put the fedora on his head, and then hesitated for a moment looking at Dee.

"Thanks for everything, Dee."

She moved closer to him. "Would ya like me to come in?" Her words froze and surrounded his face.

"You bet! Stay close. I have a feeling my mother wants to bend my ear. She likes you, you know."

"I know. Let's get inside before they find our frozen carcasses in the snow bank." She shuffled across the icy walk toward the house.

The house was a tri-level with a two car attached garage and a breezeway connecting the two, situated on a sloping landscaped yard on a two acre lot. The front yard was a good distance from the sidewalk to the house with old growth oaks and maples on either side. Karl remembered all the leaves he had to rake. He and his brother would pile them as high as they would go, tie a rope from a large branch, and with a running swing, fly through the air and land in the pile. He thought of the winter, as it was now, with the long sidewalk and curving driveway that would fill with snow to his waist, and he and his brother would have to shovel it by hand, only to have the snow plow bury the end of the drive just after they had finished the job. He smiled at how they had thrown snowballs at the plow driver.

The trees were naked now and gave no indication of the summer shade they provided or the splendid colors of fall. Suspended death.

Dee was at the porch. "By the way, Mister Germany. That hat won't cut it around here."

Karl smiled as he started toward the house. "It's a fedora."

"Whatever. You're still gonna lose your ears with that thing."

Inside, nearly every light was on. It was as if the brightness would mollify the guests' fear of death. His brother Danny was on the phone in the foyer and simply nodded as Karl headed up the stairs toward his old bedroom on the second level.

Dee followed him into the room and closed the door behind her. She remembered as teens doing the same thing. They would experiment with each others' body on the very bed she now sat upon. They would kiss for hours. He would fondle her young, perky breasts, and she would feel for the first time a young man's firmness.

"This bed brings back a lot of good memories, ya know," she said, bouncing up and down on the squeaky mattress.

He plopped his small bag on the floor. "Yeah, we had a few romps on there," he said. "My mother was so naive. She actually believed we were studying."

"We were. Anatomy." She laughed childishly.

He sat on the bed next to her. Her eyes gazed at him. She wanted to be that young girl again. Feel his lips embracing hers. Feel her full breasts against his strong chest. Feel every part of him. Feel him caress her with patient anticipation.

Karl had always been physically attracted to Dee. That had never been a problem. The problem came while he was in his last year of college, when all that seemed to remain was passionate sex. Which wasn't bad, but he wanted more. He had to move on and Germany was more of a destination of mind than location. She had always supported his lust for skiing, following him as far as Colorado once and never really enjoying her absence from home. His writing was never understood, for it was something that shouldn't come from him.

They both heard the sound of numerous voices coming through the front door.

"Did you see my dad at the funeral home?"

She shook her head. "No. Your mom said he was in a back room talking with Mister Blakemore."

"Does Blakemore still work with your dad?"

"Yeah, he's a full partner now. Handles mostly contracts."

"I pity his job. Uncle Jack kept horseshit records. He used to always say that wills were for people with relatives who didn't give a shit about anything but themselves."

"My dad had a will for me as soon as I was old enough to sign my name," she said. "I guess that says something about him."

"That's different. He's a lawyer. They're all anal."

The noise downstairs was becoming boisterous as more friends and relatives came from the funeral home.

Dee put her hand on his leg. "Do ya suppose we should go out?"

Reluctantly he rose from the bed. "I guess."

She stopped him before he got to the door. "You know you can stay with me if you want."

He didn't want to say no, outright. In fact he would have felt far more comfortable at her place than even his old bed. He was always restless here, like an animal on display to gawking patrons with self-serving motives, wanting nothing more than to throw him peanuts until he puked. He scanned the small room and noticed that even the sports posters were still taped to the walls, faded from years of sun exposure. Then he saw something shiny reflecting from a crack in a partially open closet door. He went over and slid the door wide open. The reflection came from a pair of racing skis, the bindings glistened as if new from the overhead light. He had forgotten that they were still there, the skis he had injured his knee with just before the Olympics, crushing his dream. He ran his hand up and down the smooth red, white and blue surface as if he were caressing the beautiful body of a woman. He had never raced with them again, never even taken them out for recreational use. It was as if they had somehow failed him and he hadn't wanted to reward them. He knew his crash could never be blamed on an inanimate object, like blaming a hammer for smashing a thumb, but he also knew that maintaining an edge in racing was at least fifty percent psychological, and without total faith in his equipment, he would be lost. He felt his knee ache now as if somehow it too realized it was in the presence of an enemy wanting to do it harm.

Dee came up behind him, put her hands on his shoulders, and nuzzled her head next to his. "Those are your old racing skis? The ones you . . . ."

He turned away from the closet toward her. "Yeah, I don't know why I just didn't sell them or throw them away."

She reached over and kissed him on the lips quickly as if nothing had ever changed between them. "They mean something to ya."

"Yeah, pain," he muttered.

"Please keep them. I was always so proud of you after you won a race and lifted them high above your head as though you were raising the sword that had just slain the dragon."

Now he kissed her gently, lingering as they had in the past. "We better go. My mother is waiting to chew my ass for some reason."

"Remember what I said about staying with me. I mean it."

He smiled and nodded.

CHAPTER 13

VEGETABLES AND WOODEN DUCKS

Karl's mother sprinted hastily between the dining room and the kitchen unwrapping casseroles, searching for serving spoons, and stopping from time to time wondering what she had been racing for next. Her sister Claudia was doing the same thing, with far less grace. Yet, none of the guests were in any great hurry to eat anything. It was nine in the evening and most had congregated at the bar in the basement. The older crowd sat in the dining room and lined the living room in borrowed folding chairs with their plates on their laps, nibbling cookies, and sipping decaf coffee.

Karl came into the kitchen silently from the back entrance as he had so many times in his youth for a midnight snack, and stood against the far wall watching his mother and aunt. He never understood their relationship. Aunt Claudia's husband had been in the Marines and unfortunately died in a nameless skirmish that hadn't qualified as a war. But he was dead nonetheless. She had moved back to Heiland from California after his death, bought the house two blocks away, and had never put any great effort into remarrying. She had somehow considered the idea unfaithful. She spent most days now with his mother in a brand of conversation that to outsiders would appear as rude and overly critical—a conflictive equilibrium that balanced on verbal affronts and terminating glances. But they had been that way as long as Karl could remember, and it was apparent that without that sharp edge of borderline anger they would both shrivel up and die of boredom.

He tried to smile when his mother realized he was there. She quickly reattached a piece of hair that had fallen from the top of her head. She glared at him, and he knew she was rehearsing in her mind some grand line of questioning. She had always done that, as if by hesitating the impact of her words would compound in value.

"Everything looks nice, mom."

"Nobody's eating a thing," she whispered loudly.

"They'll eat tomorrow after the funeral."

"I suppose."

Claudia came back in the kitchen, noticed the two of them together, and hastily retreated to the dining room.

"Where's Dee?" his mother asked.

"She's downstairs talking with Laura."

"Dee's a wonderful girl, ya know." She said the words as if she were lecturing him on the attributes of drinking milk. Drink from Dee. She's good for you.

"I know she is, mom. She's my best friend in Heiland."

His mother went to the cutting board, picked up a huge knife, and started chopping broccoli. "You could do worse than marry your best friend," she said.

"And if my best friend was a man?"

"You know what I mean!" she yelled softly. "Besides, people have thought a that, ya know."

Maybe that would have been easier. Simply say he was gay and she could pray for him and make everything better.

"Mom, I'm not ready to marry. I have nothing to offer anyone at this point."

She stopped chopping to stare at him. "You could teach like Uncle Jack."

"Teach where?" he said. "Jack had a PhD and regretted having gone so far in education."

She pushed a cauliflower onto the block and whacked right through it like a guillotine severing a head. "He did not!"

"The hell he didn't. We discussed it many times. He said he should have stopped with the bachelor's or master's. Anything beyond that was overkill."

"How can ya say that. He was a wonderful teacher."

"He was the best professor I ever had. But that's not the point, mother. He learned to accept it. He wanted to write, but by the time he finished his PhD there was nothing original left in his mind."

She thought for a moment carefully. "You could write here."

"Maybe after a frontal lobotomy."

Her knife chopped furiously, sending cauliflower flying everywhere. "What's wrong with here?"

"It's not just location. It's a state of mind. I could be here, but my mind wouldn't be. I need to experience Europe now while I'm young."

He turned away from her, wanting to escape back to his room. Wanting to flee even farther back to Munich. He stopped and thought for a moment. He had to do this now, or he would never make her understand anything. He turned slowly to confront her, and calmed himself inside.

"There's this little church in a small dorf on the border of Austria that I go to once in a while. It's over four hundred years old. Mozart performed there when he was sixteen. My God, there's not a structure in this country that old. Indians were still living in teepees and picking meat out of their teeth with tiny bones back then."

She pointed the knife at him. "But—"

He forged ahead. "I sit in those smooth wooden pews and I can almost feel the power of his presence. It's said that Goethe went there in his early twenties, saw Mozart play, and dreamed of bringing the Faust legend to life on the stage. It's just overwhelming to think that I might have sat in the same spot as Goethe."

His mother stared at him blankly, as if he had just recited a German poem. Then she turned back to her vegetables. "There's nothing wrong with new," she said defiantly.

"That's the whole point. There's nothing wrong with new. Do I have to do something just because everyone else is doing it? Let those who can't write, teach. We need good teachers. But let those who can write, write. Jack knew that he could write once, but that gift was gone and it killed him day after day. He didn't want that to happen to me. He wanted me to give it my best shot. I'm doing that."

"Wouldn't it be better to write full-time?"

"Of course. But I have to pay my bills."

Neither of them were aware that their voices had risen. Claudia came back into the kitchen and tried to hush them, but Karl's mother fended her off with a dramatic wave of the knife, so her sister escaped once again through the swinging door.

"You've been in Germany for over three years. Haven't ya seen enough? You could always go back on vacation."

He felt like beating his head against the wall. He knew this conversation had been brewing for three years and he dreaded the thought of it actually occurring. He could never win without completely alienating himself from her.

"It's not the same," he finally said.

"I don't understand ya, Karl. Your brother and sister both have fine, respectable jobs. There's nothing wrong with conventional."

Karl tried to stop himself, but it was no use. He was steaming now. "Danny is a Goddamn bookkeeper and Laura is a clerk at the county courthouse. Laura hates her job. Nothing changes from day to day. The same old paperwork. She's a bureaucrat. Danny looks after other people's money and wishes he had some of it. He probably likes his work because it makes him feel good to screw the government out of tax dollars by shifting the paper mill's money into different accounts. And let's face it, they haven't actually done all that well in the love and marriage department."

She turned the knife on him again, her arms flailing in the air. "That's not fair!" she yelled. "Wanda was always a . . . . Danny shoulda never married her. Laura and Will are another story. I still haven't found out what happened with them. And Danny is an accountant."

"He's not even a CPA. Besides, accountant, bookkeeper, electrician. What's the difference? The point is they are not all that happy with their lives. I'm happy."

It had actually come down to that. Comparing lives as though they were discussing elementary school grades. He never wanted it to reach that point.

She looked at him now as a mother would to a murderer son behind bars. Tears had formed at the insides of her eyes and she wiped them away briskly with a towel as if leaving them would destine her to failure. She tried to chop the vegetables, but the knife would barely slice through.

"I don't want to fight. I just got here."

He knew they would never discuss this again. That's how they were in his family. Things would churn and boil inside until finally the pressure cooker would blow its top. Then there would be uncomfortable glances for weeks, barely a word spoken, until another issue would supplant the prior one.

She took in a deep breath and recovered herself. "Have ya talked with your father?"

"No. I didn't see him at the wake."

"He was talking with the lawyer."

"Did dad make all the funeral arrangements?"

"Most of them. Uncle Jack had a will with almost everything spelled out."

"A will? He used to say . . . ." He trailed off without finishing. "Where's dad?"

"Where do ya think?"

"The shop? With all these guests?"

"Afraid so."

Karl slowly walked out into the dining room. Aunt Claudia, sitting in a chair in the corner of the room, gave him a painful smile as he passed. Finally a few people had built an appetite and were picking over the food.

Heading straight for the basement, Karl found Dee and Laura sitting on stools behind the bar mixing drinks as best they could. Karl grabbed a bottle of beer from the old refrigerator behind the bar and took a long swig. Then he reached his head over and kissed Dee on the lips quickly. He whispered in her ear, "I've gotta go talk with my dad. I'm going in."

She raised her brows and tried to smile. "Good luck."

It was common knowledge in the Schwarz household that when Frederick Schwarz, Karl's father, was in his shop he wasn't to be disturbed. The shop had become a haven from any problem for as long as Karl could remember. The shop was in the far back corner of the basement, without windows, and nearly soundproof from the entire house. Frederick Schwarz had built it himself with the sound specifications one of his major features.

Karl entered quietly and closed the door behind him. It seemed as though nothing had changed, but he was sure that it had. The two corner walls, that were front structural cement blocks covered with Styrofoam insulation and paneling, were still lined from corner to corner with three-level bookshelves. But there were only a few reference books in the room. The shelves displayed dozens of carved wooden ducks, decoy size, lifelike images in full color. Every detail down to tiny pinfeathers were meticulously and accurately depicted.

He watched his father sitting at a sturdy wooden table, a bright lamp focused on the chunk of wood in his large hands, the sharp bevel cutting tiny slivers that would be the bird's wing feathers, and Karl realized anew where much of his youth had escaped him. It wasn't as though Karl had cared to change what had been preordained, with his own preoccupation with sports and girls, but he had often wondered how things might have been different had his father been less obsessed with his wooden ducks.

Karl noticed his father's body seemed to have shrunk, with his shoulders hunched over. His head, receding with streaks of gray, was far too large for his body, as if God had made a mistake. His father would never make the same mistake with his ducks. They were perfect.

After finishing a delicate cut, his father pushed his wire-rimmed glasses farther up his nose and lifted his head up toward Karl. Although older than Uncle Jack by almost six years, his face appeared much younger. There were few wrinkles in a face that rarely smiled or depicted even curiosity or wonder through expression. It was a face that had lived an agoraphobic existence, the pale smooth skin preserved for an existential re-emergence. And it had always been a face difficult for Karl to read. Now was no exception.

"I didn't see you at the wake," Karl said, moving closer to the work bench.

His father stared blankly at him. "I was in the back taking care of some business." He paused for a moment. "Have you lost weight?"

Karl hadn't thought about it since he didn't have a scale in Germany, but when he assessed himself now the possibility did exist. "I don't know. Maybe."

"Don't they feed you over there?"

"They would be me, dad. I eat." He wasn't sure where this was leading, or why.

"Your mother worries about you," he said, changing subjects as always, almost as quickly as he changed blades while carving.

"Some things never change, I suppose," Karl said. "She'll probably be worrying about her children when she's ninety-five and Danny's seventy-five."

"How are things in Germany?"

"Fine." He knew his father was asking more because he was expected to ask than for any real concern. When his father just stared at him, Karl added, "My job keeps me busy. I seem to be on the road more than not. But that's what the job is." He looked at his father and wondered, as he had many times in the past, how he and Jack could have been brothers. Then he thought about himself and his brother Danny and it became clearer. Genes are strange things indeed.

"Are you still skiing?" he asked, with a sardonic tone.

"Till human voices wake me, and I drown," Karl said.

His father glared at him quizzically.

"Yes, until the day I die," Karl said.

Frederick Schwarz leaned back in his chair, crossed his arms, and studied his son.

Karl went over to a lower shelf and admired one of the ducks he hadn't seen before. It was a beautiful Red-breasted Merganser with a green head and red eyes and fully extended head plumage. The tiny pin feathers on its chest, brown with black specks, were so detailed the duck appeared to be stuffed or at least frozen in time. His father had gotten better over the years, he thought.

"This is a nice Merganser," Karl said.

His father swiveled in the chair. "I just finished it last week."

His father displayed only two ducks at a time upstairs on the fireplace mantle. He would change them out monthly, and only Karl would notice. To others a duck was a duck.

Karl made a move toward the door, but his father stopped him by asking, "How long will you stay?"

"I have to be back in less than six days. I have to give a city tour in Austria and Switzerland."

His father nodded. "That should be nice."

"I think so."

"See you in the morning, son."

Karl nodded and left. Outside the door he could hear the muffled laughs of people in the bar area down the hall. He felt strange about the conversation he had just had. It had seemed much more civil than any he could remember. As if his father had died too and was trying to atone for things he had done in the past. He slowly walked toward the bar, confused.

CHAPTER 14

FUTILITY

Karl went directly to the end of the bar by the fireplace, where a small fire was keeping the room warm.

He leaned against the bar and put his arm around his sister Laura, who had moved to the outside of the bar.

Laura was wearing a black dress similar to the one Dee wore, only his sister's dress was hiked up her crossed legs nearly exposing her buttocks, and the straps kept dropping off her shoulders allowing her breasts to fall to the bar and almost out for everyone to see.

But the bar had nearly emptied out by now anyway. There were a few second cousins down on the other end trying to catch a glimpse of his sister's breasts, but Dee kept distracting them by slapping them across the head. The cousins were from Minneapolis, and Dee assured them that all the girls up north smacked the men affectionately across the head. Karl guessed they liked it from the way they laughed when she did it.

His brother Dan was on the other side of Laura,

slurping the last drops from a can of Hamm's, and then seeing how loud he could burp.

"I'm really sorry about you and Will," Karl whispered into his sister's ear.

She glanced sideways at him. "Don't be, Karl. He was an asshole. We shoulda never gotten married. He was the damn high school quarterback. I shoulda known he was a faggot. Are my tits still nice? Will said they were sagging already. But feel those. These aren't saggy breasts." She grabbed his hand and placed it on her right breast, and he quickly pulled it back.

He hesitated for a moment, looking at her serious expression. She really wanted an answer. "Those are fine breasts, Laura. What does Will know?"

"Exactly. He's probably suckin' someone's dick as we speak. What does he know about tits? That's what I keep saying. That's what I told Dee. Didn't I Dee?"

Dee slapped the cousins again and said, "Right."

Laura turned back toward Karl. "What about my ass?" She swung her bottom toward Karl.

This conversation was going in the wrong direction. She was totally wasted, and he suspected he would end up hauling her up to her bedroom shortly, where she would throw up all over herself. He forced his eyes to look at her butt. "That's nice," he said.

"Just nice? Go ahead and feel it." She pulled his hand to her right cheek, and he again pulled it away.

"Very firm," he said. "You must work out a lot."

She nodded her head, and it seemed to keep going uncontrollably, like a little dog head in the back window of a car. “Aerobics. Every day. No shit.” Her eyes seemed to roll back in the sockets.

Karl motioned for Dee to come over. “Can you get her upstairs?”

“I’ve been trying for the last half hour,” Dee said.

Unfortunately, it was up to him then. Without saying a word, he helped her from the bar stool and up stairs. Her legs were wobbling and she kept asking Karl if he really thought her breasts and ass were nice. Upstairs, he sneaked her as quietly as possible through the foyer and up to the second floor. He got her to her room and set her on the bed. Then he went to close the door, and when he turned around she was standing again, with her dress pulled down in the front exposing her bare breasts.

“See. I told ya they weren’t saggy,” she slurred.

“Yes. They’re outstanding breasts,” Karl said, walking toward her. “Now you need to get to bed or all the earth’s gravity will pull on those wonderful breasts of yours and make them droop.”

“Really?” she slurred.

“Really.”

She stood with a stupid look on her face, her head cocked to one side.

Karl felt sorry for her. She didn’t deserve to feel the way she felt at such a young age. Usually married couples waited until their early forties before they could no longer stand each other and needed to move on and find themselves. Maybe Laura was better off in a way. She was still young. She could recover. Pull herself out of this self-deprecating angst.

“Let’s get this dress off,” Karl said. He slid her

dress down over her hips and she stepped out of it, almost falling to the floor. He set her back onto the bed, took off her high heels, and then slipped off her panty hose. He put her under the covers and hoped she would be all right. He'd have to check in on her before he went to bed.

When he got to the door, he could hear her mumbling about her breasts—how Karl said the earth's gravity would make them sag. She had to lay down now.

Karl quietly left and went back downstairs to the bar. He sat next to his brother, who had a new beer now. Dee was still smacking the cousins across the head, with the both of them laughing every time she did it.

"Will she live?" Dan asked, and then burped.

"Yeah. I'll check on her later."

"I can do it," Dan insisted.

"That's okay, Danny. I promised her I'd take care of her tonight."

"That's nice, Karl. But what about a week from now? Who's gonna watch over little sis then?"

Dee handed Karl a bottle of beer. It was cold and the green bottle was wet. He took a long gulp while he digested what his older brother had just said. Laura was an adult. Was it anyone's right to intrude on her life? People had to decide for themselves when enough was enough. They had to choose when they had crossed the line of ruin, and when it was time to ask for help. Maybe his sister was asking him now. Or perhaps she was too drunk to know the difference.

"Hey der, Karl," Danny said, a serious look on his

face and waving his cousins into the conversation. "Ya know what dey call second cousins in Minnesota?" When nobody answered, Danny said, "Brothers and sisters." He laughed along with his cousins until tears came to his eyes.

Karl waited and then changed the subject. "What's with the paisley, Danny?"

His brother recovered and looked at his own shirt. It was hanging out of his pants in a few places, with his gut exposed over his belt. He tried to tuck it in. "What's wrong with paisley?" He took another drink of beer from the can.

"Nothing," Karl said.

"Paisley's perfect, ya know," Dan said. "You can wear it anywhere. It's kinda like a suit, but less formal. Look at the fine workmanship on the seams. Look at this pattern. Hell, this thing cost me twenty bucks. I hear ya can get laid in Europe for that. That true?"

Karl smiled at Dee, who returned it. "I wouldn't know. I don't buy women."

"Fuuuck you. Men have bought and sold women for millions of years. It's a fact. I read it somewhere."

"Ah, then it must be true."

"Exacafuckintootly!" Danny sucked down the last of his beer, and then took in a few deep breaths before coming out with a tremendous belch. "Oh, yeah!"

Karl checked his watch. "On that note, I shall retreat." He nodded to Dee, who gave the two cousins one last slap across the head before meeting Karl around the end of the bar. Karl slapped his brother on the shoulder. "You make sure these assholes find their way to the car. And that they're riding with someone else."

His brother Dan gave him a thumbs up, and Karl and Dee went upstairs to the foyer.

Karl helped her on with her coat.

"You can still come home with me, ya know," she said, smiling.

"I'm tempted. But I'm afraid I'd miss out on the wonderful bathroom and kitchen ballet in the morning." Karl tied the wool belt around her full-length coat.

She pulled her hair out from under the collar. "Remember. Anytime."

Karl kissed her on the lips, and she pulled him closer to her, making it last longer.

"I hate you, Karl," she said seriously. "You get ta escape."

"You're a damn good friend," he said. "I don't know why you put up with my family."

"You. Do I need any other reason? Laura is fine, she just needs a big brother to straighten her out."

"And Danny?"

"You know Danny," she muttered in a resistant tone. "Please look in on Laura tonight. Don't want her ta choke on her own puke."

Karl agreed with a quick nod.

"I'll see ya in the morning," she said, kissing him again. Then she turned and went out into the frozen air.

On his way to his bedroom, Karl went into Laura's room and found her quiet and sleeping soundly with the covers up under her chin. He gently brushed her hair out of her eyes, and then kissed her on the forehead. As he left her there, she started snoring like a sailor.

CHAPTER 15

THE FUNERAL

In the morning Karl woke up with a throbbing head as if he had a hangover. But he knew it was merely a result of the long flight, long day, and inescapable discord he had experienced since his arrival in this place.

The entire family scurried about the house unaware of each other's moves, having not been together as a group for so long, and eventually reached some sort of symmetry. Aunt Claudia had arrived so early that it seemed like she had never left.

Dee O'Brien had agreed to come by to pick up Karl and drive him to the funeral. He had asked his mother if she minded, knowing that she would agree to anything that would bring the two of them closer together.

Dee had just arrived now, was taking her long wool coat off and placing it on the wooden coat tree behind the front door. She smiled at Karl as he came from his upstairs bedroom. She wore a long black dress resting conservatively on her thin ankles. Her hair was pulled up on one side exposing a tiny ear as if begging him to nibble the little lobe as he had in the past.

He came down and met her at the door, kissed her on both cheeks, and hugged her briefly. “You look really nice,” Karl said.

She blushed. “Thanks.”

He looked at himself. He wore a T-shirt and sweats, having not changed yet. His hair was still wet from his shower. “Think this will do?” he asked.

She looked him up and down. “Looks fine to me.”

He guided her up to his bedroom and closed the door behind them. He turned to her and said, “I’m going nuts, Dee. I’m not sure if I can stay here.”

She straightened her dress as she sat on the bed. She wanted him to stay with her, and had a feeling he wanted to also. But she didn’t want to sound too eager. “I’m sure your mother wouldn’t mind if you came to stay with me for a few days.”

“True. But what about us? How do we handle it?”

She thought for a long moment. “You admit you’re out of practice.” She smiled at him.

“Yeah, but remember last time? Things got a little intense.”

She kissed him quickly. “No, I did. I’m older and wiser now. I don’t think that just ‘cause ya have sex you’re connected for life. So, get dressed, Mister Germany.”

“Promise not to look?”

“Nothing I haven’t seen before.”

After he was dressed, they went downstairs where Karl told his mother they would meet them at the funeral home, and then they went out into the cold morning air. The clear frozen night had left intricate frost swirls on all the windows. Even though Dee parked her car in a garage, hers had frosted slightly on the drive over. It was twenty below zero without the wind, and that had started to pick up as they got into Dee's car.

When they got to the funeral home there were already a number of cars in the parking lot. It was quarter to ten and the funeral would start in fifteen minutes. They stepped out and stood for a moment in the cold.

"I don't understand why this isn't at the church," he said.

"The Heiland Catholics are from the old school. Ya can't go shootin' yourself."

"But it's okay to suffer?"

"Apparently. Speaking of which, it's freezing out here. And I'm not wearing pants."

They shuffled across the icy parking lot.

"Why in the hell do people live up here?" Karl asked.

"Because we're flippin' idiots. Come on."

Inside the funeral home things had changed a bit from the night before. There were more flowers. The room was filling up quickly. An organist was playing some awful tune that could only add to the anguish that most would soon feel.

The casket was closed as Karl and Dee walked by, arm in arm, to take a seat in the alcove off to the right of the main room. There were about twenty red velour chairs, and they sat in the middle row. They held each other's hand and didn't speak for a long while. The organist switched songs as though she were completing a medley of distressful standards.

After a while, Karl's family started streaming in and taking seats in front of him and around him. His mother and father and aunt Claudia sat in front and to the left of him. His sister sat next to him, patted him on his leg. She had sunglasses on, covering her bloodshot eyes. His brother Danny, after a bit of confusion, sat in front next to Claudia.

Karl recognized a number of professors; some he had taken classes from and others he had met at college functions.

The service was pretty much as Karl expected. He despised much of what was said. The minister, not knowing any better, had referred to Uncle Jack frequently as Jonathan. Although that was the name on his birth certificate, and now his death certificate, Jack hadn't been called that since youth, and only then by his mother when angry.

After the service some people hurried out to continue their lives and smoke cigarettes, while others stayed behind to give their condolences to the family. Karl had remained with Dee away from all the commotion. Then he saw someone who he thought he knew but wasn't sure. He looked like Uncle Jack's son, Geoffrey. The man was dressed rather shabbily in blue jeans and a wrinkled tan shirt with no tie. He did wear an old tweed jacket, but the leather patches on the sleeves had worn through. His long black hair lay past his shoulders in a crumpled condition. He was slowly working his way through the crowd toward the family as if stalking his prey.

Geoffrey Schwarz stepped up next to his uncle, Karl's father, and began to talk. The conversation appeared casual at first and then quickly changed.

Geoffrey started pointing his finger and his face showed reddened anger.

"I better go see what's going on," Karl said to Dee, leaving her by herself.

He walked up next to his mother, who had a tear in her eye, and asked, "What's the matter?"

Geoffrey quickly turned on him. "What's the matter? As if you don't know, asshole." Now his finger pointed toward Karl's chest.

Karl wasn't about to challenge his cousin right in front of his uncle's coffin. "What's your problem, Geoff?"

"You're my problem," he screamed. "My father never gave a shit about me because of you. You stole him while he was alive, and now you'll even take him in his death."

Karl had no idea what he was talking about. He looked at his father for help, but only got a blank stare in return. "Do you know what in the hell he's talking about, dad?"

His father hesitated for a second. "It's not something we should discuss here and now. Geoffrey, if you'd like to come by our house in a few minutes we could sit down like two rational adults and perhaps come to terms with some of what's bothering you."

"Fuck you!" Geoffrey yelled. "You can talk rationally with my lawyer." He turned quickly and stormed out of the funeral home.

"Dad, what's his problem?" Karl asked.

His mother turned away and went over to Claudia. His father shook his head. "Let's talk at home. This isn't right." His father went over to talk with a few relatives whose names Karl could no longer remember, or maybe never really knew.

Dee came up and put her arm around his waist. Together they went and talked with a few professors. One, a Dr. James, who had been Uncle Jack's closest friend on the staff and shared his lust for expatriate authors, singled Karl out at the end of the group discussion. Dee was still there, but she remained silent.

Dr. James was in her mid-thirties, unmarried, except for her literature, and had a peculiar form of speech that had always intrigued Karl. When she wanted to stress a particular point, she raised her chin and closed her eyes, as if she were making love to the words and was about to climax. She had been a frequent member of the small clan that would sit around Uncle Jack's house discussing works in progress and literature each was currently devouring. They'd go through many bottles of wine and elaborate on anyone from Joyce to Kafka to Fitzgerald. There was always work in progress, but never much completed.

Dr. James wore a long gray skirt, matching gray jacket, and a white satin shirt that buttoned up the front. It had always been difficult to imagine what lay beneath her conservative clothes, but it was likely not unappealing. If she had only found a way to shed the thick glasses and grow her hair out a bit, her fascination would have been even greater.

"How is your writing, Karl," she asked now, her eyes closing ever so slightly.

"I think I'm finding my voice," he said cautiously. "It's difficult to maintain a serious vein, one that can sustain itself over a longer work, when the writing is disjointed and interrupted."

"That's the problem, though. Sustaining the passion long enough to complete the task at hand." Her eyes closed now for a longer period.

"It's not a problem with short fiction," he explained. "That can come fast and furious and forceful. But with the novel, you must move more gently. Caress the words slowly and build up cautiously, carefully in a great crescendo until that final moment of climax."

Her eyes appeared half closed. "Yes, yes I agree."

"With work, of course, that's more difficult. But not impossible."

"Jack said you were still living in Munich and working for a tour company," she said, her eyes open now. "That should give you plenty of subjects."

Finally, he was beginning to feel comfortable for the first time since arriving in the States. He had always thought of the people on his tours as future subjects to be combined in some strange amalgamation and would eventually reincarnate as characters in short stories or his novels. And his tours were, like everything else in life, simply experiences waiting to be written about. Life was always at least two years ahead of his writing. "Exactly!" he finally said. "I meet some interesting people."

"I've always wanted to do what you're doing. You live such an interesting life. And Jack was so proud of you. You're doing something he always wanted to do also. He envied you."

Karl felt a bit strange now. He wasn't sure if he should feel guilty or glad. But he was certain she meant what she said, and that his uncle had relayed those feelings to her at some time. Dr. James had always been up front with her criticism and praise, professionally and personally.

"How long will you be in town?" she asked.

"I leave in five days."

"Perhaps we could get together and discuss some of your work," she said, her eyes closing slightly as she glanced toward Dee.

He had introduced Dee as a friend, but he wasn't sure how Dr. James had taken that. A friend could mean nearly anything. And perhaps her offer was simply a cordial gesture without hidden meaning. But he could tell, at least by Dee's disturbed look, that she had taken the invitation as something more than it was. He finally said, "Perhaps."

Dr. James reached out her hand to shake. Karl took her hand and felt a soft, warm squeeze that lingered for a moment. Then the professor slipped away to talk with one of her colleagues.

Dee took Karl's arm and led him from the funeral home. "She's gotta be wet by now," Dee murmered.

The air had warmed a bit outside, with the sun shining brightly, but the slight wind still brought a tingle to any exposed skin. They were the first ones to make it back to his parent's house. Karl suspected there would be a larger crowd than the night before. It was eleven thirty now, but he popped the top on a bottle of beer and gulped down a third.

He watched Dee watch him, unsure what was going through her mind. He wanted to be back in Munich on his rotten sofa, his computer on, and the fedora on his head bringing brilliant thoughts to his mind. Instead, he sat drinking a beer looking at a beautiful woman who probably had more feelings for him than him for her, in a house that had once been his home but now felt like a hellish prison. And all at once these feelings of guilt for not being able to accept things so simply.

CHAPTER 16

JACK'S WILL

Karl had just finished his beer when he heard the door upstairs slam and footsteps coming down the basement stairs. His father appeared at the bottom of the stairs, gave him an uncertain glance, and then nodded his head toward the wood shop in the back.

"This oughta be good," he said to Dee, leaving her alone at the bar.

When Karl got back to the shop, closed the door, and studied his father carefully, he realized the man appeared different from any other time he had seen him. His normal solemn face had actually shown concern or incertitude or maybe distress. Karl could only speculate which one.

His father took a seat in his normal wooden swivel chair as he would to carve a duck. But instead of a tool in his hand, he held a small package of papers.

It was one of those moments where his father had no clue how to proceed, Karl could tell. Yet, he had a feeling what was coming.

"What's up, dad?"

His father fumbled with the folder in his hands and then withdrew some papers. First, he spread out six pieces of official-looking papers on the work bench and evened out the creases. Then he said, "This is your Uncle Jack's will. He made me the executor." He paused for a second. "I'll let you read it in a moment, but I'll just summarize." His father pushed his glasses up on his nose. "He left you everything."

Karl couldn't believe what he had just heard. Everything? "Why?"

His father shook his head. "Geoffrey, as you know, was into drugs. Probably still is. Jack could never understand him. How he could waste himself that way. Over the last couple of years they haven't even talked. I was really surprised to see him at the funeral. But somehow he caught wind of the will, and he's going to give you trouble over it."

"It's not that important to me, dad. I thought he would give everything to you, since you were his only sibling. I thought maybe he'd give me his collection of literature, since I enjoyed borrowing his books so often."

"I don't need anything, Karl. He wanted you to write. I guess he figured this would give you a boost in life. Make you less dependent on your job. Give you more time to write."

Karl hadn't even considered this. He picked up the will and quickly scanned it, flipping through the pages. When he was done, he merely folded the paper up and set it back on the table. He couldn't help feel a little strange. There was no mention of his own son, Geoffrey. He tried to put himself in his shoes for a minute. How would he feel? That wasn't even a fair comparison, because he never expected anything from his father either. He suspected everything in life came from hard work. Whereas Geoffrey thought that life was free for the taking. Everything should be handed to him as a right of birth.

"The insurance company won't pay off since Jack took his own life," his father said. "But there are a number of other assets. His mortgage will be paid. So you could sell his house if you like. Or you could move back here and write."

Karl felt strange. For the first time his father was actually acknowledging him as a writer. He had always considered it a hobby much like his carving of wooden ducks. But now he really considered it a possibility.

"I'm not ready to move back," Karl said. "I'm just not mentally ready." He was certain he could never live in Uncle Jack's house in Duluth.

"That's your decision, Karl." He looked at his son more critically now, and then pulled out a white envelope from the small package that had contained the will. "Jack left you a letter." He handed the envelope to Karl, which he accepted.

His father rose from his chair and headed out the door. He stopped before opening it and turned to Karl.

"Think about moving back. We'd like to see you at least once a year. And you know how we both feel about Dee." He smiled ever so slightly. It was barely visible, wouldn't have been to the casual observer, but it was a smile.

Karl didn't answer. He simply stared at his father as he left and closed the door behind him.

Flipping the letter over, he saw his name and

Munich address on the other side. There were stamps on it, but it had never been sent. He opened it slowly. There were two pages hand written on university stationary. The pen strokes were undoubtedly Uncle Jack's, a wide, indistinguishable combination of cursive and block letters. It had taken Karl some time to get used to his writing in the margins of Karl's manuscripts. The letter read:

Dear Karl,

By now I'm only a memory. I hope good. I put stamps on the envelope for legal reasons so only you could read it. It would be against federal law for others to open. I'm serious about the will. Geoffrey has never felt like my son. And knowing his mother, there is the possibility he isn't. But that doesn't matter. The will should hold up under the scrutiny of any court. I want you to know a few things about me. First of all, I am so happy and proud that you have become a writer. You're living the life that I only dreamed of. I should have never gone on for my *doctorate. It ruined me. I gained a greater appreciation for literature, perhaps, but I no longer had the ideas and objectivity required to produce quality fiction. You have that special quality. Don't ever give up. I know you can become one of America's great writers. You have the drive and dedication. The intellect. But don't let life pass you by. You know how much I enjoyed life. I'll get back to that. But don't completely shut yourself off from the world. My marriage wasn't a good example of what I'm talking about. I should have never married when I did or who I did. But don't give up on the hope of a relationship that means more than just great sex. Although, as you know, there's nothing wrong with having both. If you find that special person, don't let her get away. Love should be just like your writing. Don't let any obstacle, however grand it may seem, stand in your way. I think you know what I mean. Last of all, don't end up like me. I'm not as strong as you. I can't beat cancer. You probably could. This is no way to live. I refused the chemo because the doctors said it was most likely too late anyway. So I'm taking the easy way out. What the hell. Hemingway did it! Take care, Karl. And always remember I love you. Keep writing.*

Love, Jack

Karl finally broke down in tears for the first time since coming home. He folded the letter and put it back in the envelope. It finally hit him that all the long discussions were over. All the late-night sessions with fine wine and intellectual intercourse with Uncle Jack and the small group of professors, gone. And it was those, more than anything else, that he missed most about this place. He wiped his eyes with his shirt sleeve and took a deep breath. The letter had given him more than just hope. More than a sense of great loss. His Uncle Jack, even in death, had guided him once again in the direction he knew in his heart to be the right way. He would have to find a way, the strength, to do the right thing.

CHAPTER 17

BRUSSELS

Angelique Flaubert had postulated for two days on whether to go home for the weekend, her options really a matter of duty over personal desire. In the end, duty seemed to grasp her by the throat, as it had so many times in the past, and she found herself packing a small bag, reluctantly, picking up a night train from Munich to Brussels, and sat now at a window seat as the train slowed for the outskirts of Brussels.

The sun was rising, bringing a cold yellow hue to the track-side of old brick apartments. She wanted to remain on the train when it stopped, or quickly catch a train in the opposite direction. But the apprehension she felt would never go away, she knew, until she faced it head on. She still wasn't certain what she would do or if she would ever find the courage to do what she wanted. She only knew that to not try was to fail.

The train slowed to a crawl and came to an abrupt halt at the central train station near the Royal Museums of Fine Art. She caught a glimpse of the four Corinthian columns, each topped by bronze statues, and she thought of sneaking off through a back door and spending the morning browsing through the wide corridors, admiring the paintings and sculptures. But on Saturday the museums wouldn't be open, she realized.

Dazed passengers began to rise from their chairs collecting their belongings, pushing their way to the exits. Angelique pulled her small bag from under her seat, lingered for a moment, wondering if she could possibly find a way out of what she knew to be the truth of her visit, and then gradually she rose and shuffled toward the exit.

Outside, the air was warmer than in Munich, and the smell of the sea, although miles away, seeped in with a salty, pleasurable reward. She stood on the cobblestone sidewalk as people passed around her in a hurried mass to get home or nowhere, and she realized it was the smells that she missed most about Brussels. Germany had bakeries. But there was something special about the essence of croissants floating about the streets of Brussels. Even the fresh fish markets on the narrow streets around the Grand Place, with their ubiquitous odors, would be sorely lost. It was these aromatic perfections and imperfections that would be nearly impossible to leave behind for long.

She stood gazing toward the passing cars on the Rue dus Ursulines, their horns honking as they came upon slower or halted traffic. Busses stopped at the curb and then pulled away in a plume of diesel smoke, and she thought once again of returning to the terminal and heading home to Munich.

The silver Mercedes, impeccably clean, drove up

and stopped in front of Angelique. It was her father. Even on a Saturday morning he wore an expensive gray suit, perfectly tailored to a body that had lost some of its vitality over the years.

Renault Flaubert was a tall Belgian in his mid-forties. He had married young and had just the one child, Angelique. He had been handsome, by many standards he still was, but the luster had tarnished most recently as some of his business holdings had begun to fail. His hair was more gray and less silver and black, receding back from the sides. He smiled slightly with an extended, comical jaw, as if it had been broken many times in street fights. But Renault had never been in a fight, other than verbally with a garcon over the quality of a wine.

Angelique heard the electric door lock click open as if she were a street walker being picked up by an older businessman for a sordid affair. She got in and threw her bag to the back seat.

"Glad you could come by for me, father," she said in French.

Her father stretched a painful smile and pulled out into traffic. His face was much more animated, she thought. The lines around each eye seemed to pull from the back of his head, like claws from a lion trying to tear his face in half.

After they drove for a while through heavy traffic, her father finally said, "Have you been eating properly?"

"Yes! Beer and chocolate."

"Adrien would have come for you, you know, but he was called away to business."

Called away by his father, she thought. The business would always be more important to him than she ever could become. And the children, if it ever came to that, would mean even less, unless it was a male who showed an interest in the business. The Talbots had been merchants for centuries. They had survived two world wars and Nazi occupation, some would say through collaboration, and had actually thrived. They were at one time dependent on the sea with ventures in fishing and shipping. But in the last few decades they had diversified into high technology manufacturing and hotels and had even built a golf course south of Brussels near the famous Waterloo.

"I have a feeling Adrien will come up short a lot," she finally said.

"The Talbots have important businesses. You should feel lucky you're marrying into such a family."

She looked out the window wistfully at couples walking hand in hand down the sidewalk. Happy people.

"Lucky," she murmured. "That's what I was thinking. What do the Talbots have planned for this weekend?"

He weaved through the traffic as if impervious to her question. Then he said, "We have a dinner planned for this evening. The Talbots, of course. We must plan for June."

We, she thought. He meant they. She hadn't been asked her opinion on anything, even on the selection of her spouse. The Talbot family would control the entire affair, from the color of the flowers, to the words said at the ceremony, to the location of their apartment following the wedding. They would probably even determine the frequency of sex following the consummation, she thought.

The heavy Mercedes lumbered through the traffic and then into a relatively tranquil section of town where large trees lined the wide boulevard and brick houses of old money sat back from the road at a corruptible distance. Her father pressed a button and a metal gate covered in barren ivy vines opened for them and closed as the car cleared it. He stopped just in front of the garage and left the engine running.

She took this as a sign to get out and she would see him sometime in the afternoon after he had finished playing chess, eaten lunch, filled up on drinks and conducted unofficial business at the club most of the morning.

She grabbed her bag and started to get out and then stood with the door open momentarily. "Thanks again for the ride. Sorry if I've inconvenienced you." She slammed the door and walked briskly toward the rear entrance of the house. She heard the car slowly turn around and head back down the drive and out the gate.

The house hadn't changed, although she had been home for Christmas only a few months ago. The large three-story brick building, with Roman arched windows, slate roof, and multiple gables, had been in the family for over a hundred and fifty years. The matching single-level carriage house behind was occupied by the housekeeper.

She entered through the thick wooden door that resembled one she had seen on a palace tour in Austria, she couldn't remember which one now, and went into the kitchen. She began rummaging through the refrigerator, an act that was despised by her mother, and she found an apple and a small bottle of orange juice. She sat at the table and started taking bites out of the apple when her mother came through from the dining room.

Francoise Flaubert glared and took a seat opposite her. She, like Angelique's father, was dressed for the day, as if by virtue of its relative importance to them would somehow transmute through Angelique. Her blonde hair was up high on her head as if she were ready for the evening meal. Her white silk blouse sat freshly over her firm upper body, a body she had always prided herself on. And her gray wool skirt was tight and shifted upward as she crossed her long, firm legs clad in black decorative nylons with roses and vines that streaked the length of her legs.

Angelique had always been proud of the way her mother appeared on the outside. She had waited patiently for the day when her legs were as long and firm as hers, her breasts as large and defined. And now, when that time had arrived, Angelique couldn't find the strength and pride within herself to show what she had. Instead, she sat across the table in blue jeans and a baggy sweat shirt, her long leather jacket folded over the chair to her side.

"Your father found you without a problem I see," her mother said. "Adrien wanted to pick you up, but he's at a business meeting discussing something or other." She flicked her hands as she spoke as if punctuating each sentence.

"It's not a problem," Angelique said. "I suppose I'll have to get used to it like you. Besides, I adore heedlessness." She smiled and her mother stared back at her in wonder. She knew her mother had been having affairs for years. Her mother had always thought of herself as impervious to discovery, but even Brussels had rumors that were found to be true over time. And now her mother realized that her daughter's fate would likely be the same as hers. A marriage out of convenience where love and lust were subjugated by strangers.

Her mother still stared but finally said, "Did your father mention the dinner here tonight?"

"Yes! And my appetite just took a turn for the worse."

"You still have clothes here in your room," her mother said, rising from her chair and straightening her skirt.

"That's not the problem and you know it!" Angelique screeched, as she rose to meet her mother. She pointed her finger and continued. "I haven't even kissed Adrien. Not that I want to. But you would think that there should be some intimacy prior to marriage, if not sex, to see if there is passion between two people. How could you expect a marriage to last without that?"

Her mother flipped her hands in a preemptory gesture. "It's been going on for centuries. Think of it as a . . . business arrangement."

Angelique flashed with anger, her auburn hair seemed to fill with her own blood and the vessels in her neck bulged. "Business arrangement!" she yelled. "Are you fucking crazy?"

"Watch your mouth," she screamed back.

"I will not. I can't believe my own mother would

sell me as if bartering for fish in the market. I'm not one of fathers commodities."

"I only want what's best for you," her mother pouted, her voice cracking with each word. "Adrien is a good man. You'll come to love him. You'll see."

Her mother had always equated love with time, as if the two were matched inextricably, ticking away with each second greater than the last. Perhaps love could never be the magical dream that Angelique had found it to be. Something that merely happened and there was nothing a person could do to change that fact.

"Is Eliza here?"

Her mother's head bobbed up and down. "She's up cleaning your room."

Angelique slipped out of the kitchen and went upstairs. When she entered her bedroom, she notice Eliza, the housekeeper, making her large canopy bed with spiraled oak posts.

Eliza was in her early forties, petite and pretty, and barely five feet tall. She was more like a mother or older sister to Angelique than an employee of her family.

Sneaking up behind the unassuming woman, Angelique grabbed her in the butt.

Eliza turned swiftly. "Oooo. My God!"

"Gotcha."

"This is a long weekend," Eliza said. "You have to sleep sometime, Angel."

The two of them embraced and then sat down onto the bed together.

"I didn't think you were coming," Eliza said.

"Believe me. I'm not even getting excited.

They laughed together.

Eliza narrowed her eyes at Angelique. "I've seen that look in your eyes before. What do you have planned?"

"If you know, mother will hold it against you. Tell me what you've been up to."

Rising from the bed, Eliza went to the window overlooking the back courtyard and garden. "I have a new man."

Angelique jumped from the bed and rushed to her friend. "Really? What happened to Andre?"

"I let him go. He's better off. Besides, Antonio is more . . . qualified."

"He's hung, isn't he?"

"Like a horse. And he doesn't mind if you go to the whip to make it to the wire." Eliza pranced about the wooden floor as if riding a horse.

"You're so bad. Tell me more."

Eliza turned and grinned at her. "You tell me. What about this Karl? Shetland or Thoroughbred?"

Angelique giggled. "I don't know. He has big hands."

Eliza raised her tiny hands in the air for inspection. "Have you seen Adrien's? They're like a child's. You know, if you marry him you'll need to keep a real man on the side."

"Don't even talk about that."

"Which part? Marrying Adrien, or the other?

"You're so bad." Angelique hugged her and held on tight. "I love you."

CHAPTER 18

THE RIGHT THING

Dressed only in her undergarments, Angelique swirled around her room as if she had woken from a nightmare in a strange place. The canopy bed, the matching dresser and wardrobe, were all suddenly alien to her. Evening light seeped through the tall arched windows, casting diamond-shaped shadows across the wooden floor.

Standing before a full-length mirror, she pressed a formal dress against her nakedness and pondered her impending fate. She knew the four parents would conspire against her, and Adrien, although remaining relatively quiet, would nod his agreement. She looked at the dress, a pure flowered pattern that could have been cut from the same swatch as her bed canopy. A dress her mother had purchased in her absence, she flung it hastily to the floor, went to the wardrobe, and started flipping through the items. The mini skirt? No! Nothing that would reveal anything to him. She moved to the right and found an old pair of jeans that she had brought home with her from Germany in December. They weren't faded, but they weren't new. They were at that comfortable stage, and she wondered why she hadn't brought them back to Munich with her. She put them on and added a black leather belt. Then she found a fluffy tan angora sweater. She hadn't worn it since her breasts were barely noticeable. And now, with the baggy abundance of the soft sweater, any viewer would wonder if she even had breasts. She smiled as she looked at herself in the mirror. She put on leather heal-less shoes. Italian. And pulled her hair back into an awkward ponytail. Adrien had commented once on how she should never pull her beautiful hair back and should always have it flow down over her shoulders.

Eliza came in and raised her brows seeing what Angelique was wearing.

"Everyone's here, Angel," Eliza said. "You're not wearing that?"

"You like it?"

Examining her more carefully, circling her, Eliza said, "Let me sneak out through the back door before you come down."

Angelique frowned, looking for the right answer.

"All right," Eliza said, looking her over again. "Let's see. They'll see nothing of your wonderful figure. Denim decadence. Perfect."

"Glad you like it, my dear. My people await."

Eliza left and Angelique followed her slowly down the stairs. Walking down the steps, she thought about Karl and the last time they were together. He had an understanding of her that was haunting and pure, as if her soul had seeped from her body, floating above the two of them momentarily, and then swooping down to occupy his body and make him speak what she knew to be the truth. She gained strength from her thoughts.

At the bottom of the stairs she heard talking in the library, and knew they must be sitting around with drinks discussing trade agreements that she found totally boring unless they involved her. She entered the room quietly and stood for a moment.

Mr. and Mrs. Talbot were sitting in high-back leather chairs, he impeccably dressed in an Italian suit and she in an evening dress that had been purchased vainly by size and not fit. Their backdrop was a wall of leather-bound books that had been in the family for a hundred years or more, updated from time to time with contemporary cult sensations, yet neglected more than not for less pretentious titles of nonfiction on business that remained out of sight in her father's bedroom. Her father sat behind his large oak desk in the same suit he wore when he picked her up at the train station in the morning, a glass of brandy in his left hand, and a look of repulsion on his face as he gazed at her. Now her mother, standing next to the brick fireplace in conversation with Adrien, glared at her as well.

Adrien turned to her and then headed in her direction. She quickly made her way to the small bar cabinet, ignoring his advance, crouched and lingered for a moment choosing what she wanted, and then settled on a dark Belgian ale with the highest possible alcohol content. She flipped the top and poured it slowly into a tall glass, watching the heavy head rise to the top and an anxious Adrien on the periphery.

He came closer to her now. He wore a suit that

could have been, and may have been, from the same fabric as his father's. Conservative gray with intermittent streaks of wine red like his eyes. Eyes with black centers like that of a mouse cornered momentarily in the shadows and searching for a direction to escape, shifting frequently to others in the room and never settling on the one in conversation. His preposterous jaw stretched upward at the end like a ski jump and even higher as he shifted his neck from the tight little red tie. His perfect hair, always perfect, lay smoothly back in a blinding sheen.

Finally, Adrien said, "How was your trip?"

She thought. "Which one?"

He laughed from his gut in an untimely guffaw and she cringed for having made it possible, not remembering just how repulsive it was. "Which one?" he repeated.

She took a long gulp of beer and shielded herself from the piercing eyes of her mother and especially her father who seemed to still be in shock over her appearance. She wanted to turn and quickly flee upstairs, pack her bags and hop the next train back to Munich. But even there she would be alone. Todd Stewart was somewhere in the Italian Alps freezing his behind off, and Karl Schwarz, whom she knew she needed now more than ever, was in America and for all she knew would never return. She couldn't even fathom that thought. She looked now at her future husband, his whimsical jaw, his slick hair that could lubricate a thousand autos, and she began to gain more and more strength for what she had to do. She took another long draw from her beer, finishing it.

Adrien's jaw stiffened. "We need to—"

"Talk," she said. "I know. I've been here all day."

"I was off with my father on business," he pleaded.

"A woman doesn't like to be ignored."

"So, that's what this is about." His beady eyes flipped up and down her body.

"What?"

"The clothes."

"This is the way I dress."

"In Munich, perhaps. Maybe you should move back here immediately."

Angelique pointed her beer bottle at his face. "Maybe I should cram—"

Suddenly, Eliza entered. "Dinner is served."

They all left the library, with Angelique in the rear after taking another beer bottle from the refrigerator.

She brushed by Eliza. "You just saved Adrien from a painful operation. A rectal bottle-ectomy."

"Ouch," Eliza said, closing the door after them.

When Angelique got to the dining room, everyone was sitting at the long oak table; her father on one end and Adrien's father on the other, the mothers on one side and the unlikely couple on the other. That was one small consolation, she thought. She wouldn't have to look across the table at him.

The dinner was brought out in hurried courses. First a small appetizer, stuffed olives. Then quickly a full plate of pork and potatoes with a mushroom sauce. It was at this time, with full plates and each person cutting meat vigorously, that Angelique decided would be just right.

Angelique filled her beer to the top of the glass,

pushed her chair back, rose, and said, "Mother, father, Mister and Mrs. Talbot." She raised her glass as if to toast. "Adrien. I'm sorry but I cannot possibly go through with this wedding in June. May you find it in your hearts to forgive me." She took a long, slow swig of beer, her eyes peering over the top, and then sat down.

Adrien had a piece of half-chewed pork stuck between his teeth with a clenched jaw, his fork and knife pointing in her direction as if ready and willing to strike. He swallowed the large chunk of meat. "What do you mean? Do you need more time?"

She stared at her glass, not daring to look at her mother or father, or even giving a hint as though she would acknowledge the Talbots. "More time would be nice," she said. Time for all other men on Earth to be decimated by a penis-eating disease.

"More time?" he repeated. "Would August be better?"

"Which year?" she said, trying to keep from smiling.

He guffawed again and it seemed as if large chunks of pork would come flying from his enlarged nostrils. "I get it," he finally said. "You're joking!"

Then the quiet room erupted in laughter from her parents and the Talbots. Adrien's was the loudest. She smiled and tried to pull the words from within her that the joke wasn't intentional. In fact the joke was the fact that they were engaged in the first place. Engaged to a man she had never kissed, nor desired to. Engaged to be married out of a convenience that wasn't hers but an aberration of five conspirators who thought more about choosing the right clothes than allowing nature to determine the righteousness of matrimony. She wanted to spring from her chair, throw down her fine linen napkin, storm out of the room, float to the top of the stairs, and plop down on her bed in a delirious combination of tears and laughter. She would have if her father hadn't rose from his chair at that moment raising his glass in an exalted fashion, a toast that he knew to be true to the evening's real intention. His intention. He was no longer smiling. He toasted the union of the Talbots and the Flauberts as if the two would be united in a sadistic pagan orgy and she, Angelique, was the sacrificial soul offered to an unseen deity for a desire that wasn't hers, a dream that wouldn't go away, a nebulous aspiration that would never be realized in her mind. She heard the words and stared in affronted agony but couldn't move her lips or her body to react. He had made up his mind, and hers, and she knew that his power, his strength, was far superior to hers. How could she say no? It would be an insult to the family name. A name that had transcended great obstacles in legal and literary circles of fate for centuries. She knew she couldn't fight him. And she knew that he knew she hadn't been making a joke, even though she had done similar things in the past.

She didn't utter another word through dinner. Her eyes remained on her food and drink. When they were done, the Talbots and her parents retreated to the library again. They wanted to discuss the wedding further, and what would surely come of the union. The business merger and the eventuality of children. Adrien suggested they move to a sitting room on the second floor, just two doors down from her bedroom. They sat there now quietly, not looking at each other or at anything in particular.

He sighed as though wanting to say something and then paused. He shifted his thick jaw and head to make eye contact and said, "I love you, Angelique." His words came out stilted, as if in his thirty years he had never said a less congruous set of words.

Without saying a word, she got up and went to her bedroom, locking the door securely behind her.

CHAPTER 19

AN UNDERSTANDING

"Please, Karl. Call me Emily. Dr. James is so formal."

Karl was standing in the foyer of Professor James' house two blocks from the university. Two days had passed since the funeral. Heiland's scarcity had nearly driven him crazy, so he had called her on a whim and she had asked him over to discuss his work. It was nine in the evening now, and the temperature had finally warmed somewhat, allowing it to snow.

He had never been in her house before, but it was similar to others in the neighborhood that he had seen. The house was eighty years old. Hardwood floors. Formal dining room. Plants everywhere. A cat was sitting on painted iron radiators, flicking its tail.

"Okay, Emily," he said, and then followed her into the living room.

"Would you like some wine?" she asked.

He hesitated.

"It's a French Merlot."

"Great," he agreed.

She went to the kitchen, and he watched her slip across the smooth wooden floor like she was skating across ice. She was wearing black tights that clung to her thin waist and a bulky angora sweater that showed him nothing.

He had brought a folder with a few short stories he had written recently. He set them on the coffee table and accepted the glass of wine. She sat on the sofa next to him and sipped her wine.

"This is good," he said, after tasting the wine.

"It's not bad," she agreed. "I got it in the Twin Cities. The selection here is minimal."

She appeared to be looking him over for any imperfections, much like she had when she tasted her wine.

"You wanted to see some of my works in progress," Karl said, breaking her stare.

"Yes." She picked up the first story and started reading.

Karl watched her now. He wondered why she was still single. She wasn't a raving beauty, but she was very attractive. Her large blue eyes flicked across the page as she read. She would pause for a moment to sip her wine, and then much like Angelique would do, she would lick her lips to catch any remainder. She had a cute little nose that seemed Scandinavian, turning up at the end like a ski jump.

She turned to the third page now, and Karl tried to remember what was going on in the story at that stage. How would she like his writing? She had given him favorable comments while he was a student. Yet, things had changed now. He was no longer looking for a grade, not that he ever really cared about them anyway, but more for an analysis of his strengths and weaknesses. He wasn't ready to send the story off to a magazine yet, for it hadn't aged properly. He always let his work sit for a few months before he reviewed it again to see the work fresh in his mind, as an editor would.

When she finished the ten pages, she let them hang in her limp hands for a moment, while she closed her eyes and thought of her comments.

Finally she said, "I don't understand, Karl."

He looked at her carefully, not certain what to say. "You don't like it."

"No, I don't." She hesitated. "I love it. What I don't understand, is how your fiction has improved so profoundly in such a short period."

He thought about writing the story in Munich, his fedora on the back of his head. Should he tell her about Kafka's fedora? "Thank you," he said. "It's nice of you to say that. And I respect your comments. But, is there anything you don't like?"

She considered that, her eyes nearly closed as her head moved closer to his. "It ended too soon. I think this could be a novel. Don't get me wrong, it's a wonderful short story. I just wanted more. I really liked the characters, and I think you could enhance them in a novel."

"It's interesting you say that," he said, somewhat relieved. "Because the novel I'm writing is similar to that story."

"I'd love to read it."

Karl thought about it. "I don't know. It's rough and in various stages of completion. I wouldn't feel right about you spending your time on an early draft." She looked disappointed, so Karl added, "Could I send you a copy from Germany when I'm done?"

Her eyes widened. "Would you?"

"Sure. I'll send you a copy."

She finished her wine and offered him more, and then filled both glasses three fourths full. They sat in silence for a moment. A clock ticked on the fireplace mantel.

"What are you thinking?" she finally asked.

"I was wondering if you had a boyfriend. And if not, why not?"

"Are you interested?"

Perhaps he hesitated too long. "Well. There's nothing I can do about it now. I'm thinking about someone else."

"The woman you were with at the funeral?"

How could he explain Angelique? Someone untouchable. "I'm staying with her." He paused. "We're just friends."

"You seemed like more than friends to me."

"We were at one time. But not anymore."

She finished her glass of wine and set the cup on the coffee table. Then she slowly lifted her sweater over her head, exposing her bare breasts. They were round and firm. Not huge, but not small.

Karl was somewhat shocked. "What are you doing?"

She centered her eyes on his and then let them roam across his body. "It's been a long time, Karl."

The same was true for him. He rose slowly. "I should probably get going."

"You don't like them?"

What was this with women and their breasts lately. First his sister, and now the professor. "They're really nice."

She slipped across the sofa toward him. "I need you. Right now. She ran her hand over his jeans."

"I don't think it's a good idea."

She started caressing her right breast. "Come on. It'll be fun."

"I'm sure it would be—"

"But, you're worried about Dee? Call her up. See if she'd be interested in a threesome."

He thought for a second. "You're kidding, right?"

She smiled and raised her brows.

It was hard to think of turning her down, alone or with Dee. In fact, it was just plain hard. He wasn't sure what to do.

•

On the drive back to Dee O'Brien's house, in her car, he wondered if he had made the right decision. Maybe he would never know for sure. Yet, he had a feeling his choice would come back to haunt him in the end.

He pulled into Dee's driveway and noticed another car parked out front. It was a beat up late seventies Chevy, with only rust holding it together. The trunk was held down with wire wrapped around a wooden bumper.

Heading through the front door, he immediately knew that the night had gone from strange to stranger. His cousin, Geoffrey Schwarz, was standing in the middle of the living room.

Dee was on the sofa flipping through channels on cable, trying to ignore his cousin.

"You all right, Dee?"

She nodded, but still looked annoyed.

"What are you doing here, Geoff?" Karl asked.

His cousin had been staring at him with wild, bloodshot eyes since Karl came through the door.

"I want what's mine," Geoff said. "You didn't deserve to get his stuff."

Karl swirled the car keys around his finger. How did he respond to that? "Maybe not. In fact, I didn't want anything. Maybe some of his books. There's something special about reading the same book as someone you admire. Someone who enjoyed the books so thoroughly."

"Fuck you! Jesus Christ. You even talk like the sonofabitch. Why don't you get a life?"

"You mean get high like you? So you can forget about how horseshit life has been to you. Who said life was meant to be enjoyed? Maybe God placed us here to test us. If we don't fuck up too badly, then he sends us to a better place."

"You believe in that heaven bullshit?" Geoff said.

Karl moved over toward the sofa and sat next to Dee. She still had the remote, but had settled on a cartoon network. Now the Smurfs droned their whiny little voices in the background.

"I don't know," Karl said. "I'm not sure we aren't there now. Maybe there's nothing out there." He swirled his arms toward the ceiling. "Maybe you die and simply shrivel up until all the moisture is out of you. Maybe there is no soul that escapes and reunites with others who have gone before us. I don't know."

"Would you like to find out?" Geoff slid a gun out

from his jacket. A revolver that looked like a toy and a deadly weapon, simultaneously.

Dee sat up straight. "Put that away!" she yelled.

"Fuck you, bitch."

Not sure what to do, Karl leaned back in the sofa. "Just put the gun away, Geoff."

"Give me what's mine!" he yelled, pointing the gun at Karl's head.

Karl had never been so scared and angry at the same time. He got up from the sofa and moved to the side of the table. His cousin was four feet from him. The gun only a foot or so away. "I don't want anything. In a few days I go back to Germany. I may never return."

While he and his cousin were talking, Dee slipped off to her bedroom.

"Just turn everything over to me."

"Hey, that's fine with me," Karl said. "I don't have room for anything else in my apartment anyway."

Geoffrey was thinking it over. He lowered the gun and let it hang from his flaccid arm. His eyes were fixed on the baby blue Smurfs prancing across the television screen. "I'm confused. Why don't you want my father's stuff? Isn't it good enough for you?"

Shit! Now what? There would be no reasoning with this asshole. "His stuff is fine. But you obviously need it more than I do."

"What's that supposed to mean? You think 'cause I drive that shitty old Chevy I need the money?"

"This is total bullshit."

"You got that right."

"Put the gun away. I'll get you a beer. We'll laugh

about this in the morning."

Tears streaked down Geoffrey's face and he started to sob, his eyes locked on the Smurfs. "I used to love the Smurfs," he said. "I'd roll a joint, grab some munchies, and watch them every Saturday morning."

"Hey, how do you think the Smurfs are born?" Karl asked. "There's only one Smurfette and she's gotta be a virgin."

"Some huge snake shit them out and they hatched from eggs."

"Damn! That's what my friend Todd thinks."

"Shut up!" He raised the gun again.

"Listen, this is a little intense, man."

"Maybe it's never been you. Maybe it's me."

Suddenly, the front door burst open, with one sheriff's deputy high and one low, pointing their guns right at his cousin.

"Drop the gun, asswipe!" screamed the man up high. It was the same man Karl had punched on his first night in Heiland. He still had a swollen upper lip.

Geoffrey was confused. He looked at the gun in his hand. "I drop it and you shoot me." He slowly raised the gun, being careful not to point it toward the cops.

Karl could see Dee peering through a partially open bedroom door. He nodded for her to go back inside.

"Put the gun down!" the cop yelled again.

"Fuck you." His cousin slid the gun to his own temple. "I want to see my father. Maybe things will be different."

The blast was muffled by bullet crushing skull and brains. His cousin hit the floor almost immediately. Blood splattered on the wall.

Karl turned away. He heard the sheriff's deputies kick the gun aside. Then Dee was at his side, her arms around him.

"Why'd he have to do that?"

"I don't know," she said softly. "Some people have to self-destruct."

CHAPTER 20

THE ROAD TO HEILAND

The sky was a dark blue; not a single cloud swirled about. Only a lone jet contrail gave Karl any indication on depth beyond the troposphere above the Heiland municipal hockey rink. Subsequently, the air was thin and cold. Numbingly so.

He stood in a snow bank with his sister Laura watching their brother's hockey team take on a rival team from a neighboring town.

Wearing the fedora had been a mistake, Karl knew. Maybe Dee was right; Karl would be lucky not to lose an ear.

Laura stamped her feet to life. "This is such an idiotic sport," she said. "It's twenty below and grown men with metal on their feet are trying to beat the shit out of each other. Once in a while they actually try to put this hard rubber thing into the net with sticks. Brilliant, eh?"

"Men are always trying to stick something somewhere," Karl said, shoving his hands deeper into his pockets. "Little white ball in hole. Orange ball through hoop. Oblong ball through goal posts. Black and white ball into net."

"Don't forget the hot-dog into the bun. That's what most men really want. Except for those I marry."

Karl wrapped his arm around her shoulder pulling her closer. "You'll be all right."

She swiveled her head up to him. "Youse guys think alike. Danny said the same thing."

Turning her head, she watched two men fight for the puck against the boards.

"Why didn't you try to make a comeback for the Olympic team?" she asked solemnly.

He had asked himself that same question a hundred times, with no definitive answer. Perhaps he was afraid of failing again.

"I know it's hard to understand," he said. "People come back from injuries every day, especially these days. Maybe it had nothing to do with my bum knee. Maybe . . . maybe I didn't want to dedicate four years to a goal that flew by in seconds."

"Sorry. I didn't mean to dredge up bad memories."

"It's all right, Laura. I never explained myself to anyone. In fact, you're the first person in Heiland to actually come out and ask the question. Maybe if someone had asked earlier, I would have been forced to face it sooner."

"You're still young," she said. "You're in great shape. You could try again."

He shook his head. "No. There's no desire anymore. And, really, that was the problem after the accident. I lay in my hospital bed and couldn't come up with one good reason to continue."

She nuzzled closer to him. "I wish you didn't have to leave."

"If you think I'm gonna stay back here and freeze my ass off, forget it."

Two men collided on the ice, their sticks flying across the rink.

"I don't know what to do," Laura said. "I've always had a boy friend."

"You have to live with yourself twenty-four hours a day. Once you learn how to do that, the rest is easy."

She cocked her head to one side, like she had the night she was drunk and he had put her to bed. "Okay, grasshopper."

"Bite me."

One of the hockey players scored, and they all started skating toward the two of them. They opened the wooden door and waddled through the snow to the warming house.

Danny was the goalie just scored on. He stopped by Laura and Karl and smacked a guy with his stick.

"That was a lucky shot, asshole," Danny said to the other player.

"In your dreams, Danny boy," the man said over his shoulder.

"Did you see that?" Danny asked Karl. "The puck bounced off his own man's skate. That's illegal."

Laura pulled away. "I'm gonna get some hot chocolate." She shuffled off through the snow to the warming house.

Danny pulled off his helmet and mask. "What da hell were you two talking about?"

"Trying to figure out why grown men play hockey."

"You see that goal out there?"

"Afraid not."

The two of them stared at each other uncomfortably.

"You got something on your mind, little brother. I can tell."

Karl hesitated. "I don't know. I get this feeling you're pissed off at me for some reason. What's up with that?"

Danny laughed as he leaned up against his hockey stick. "You think everything has to do with you?"

"No. I just—"

"My wife, ex-wife, is a bitch. I got a gut I can't get rid of. I'm losing my damn hair. In high school they voted me most likely to succeed. I didn't even go to college. I'm stuck in this nowhere job, still living in this podunk town. And to top it off, I got hemorrhoids the size of oranges. And you got da balls to ask me what's wrong?"

Danny pointed his stick at Karl and then poked him lightly in the chest.

"But—"

"You self-righteous little puke," Danny continued. "World traveler. Writer. You think anyone around here gives a shit about that? Fuck no! You can kiss my fat ass you little fedora-wearing prick."

Karl thought for a micro-second. He probably could've let everything pass if he hadn't mentioned the fedora. He knocked his brother's stick away and tackled him into a snow bank. Then he started punching away at his older brother. Unfortunately, with all the gear, he wasn't doing much damage.

"Knock it off!" Danny screamed.

"Fuck you! I just asked you a simple question."

Finally, Karl connected with a punch to the face, giving his brother an instant bloody nose. Exhausted, the two of them sat in the snow, breathing heavily. Karl collected the fedora, which had fallen from his head in the fracas, and he wiped some snow from the brim before returning it to his head.

"I don't get you, Karl. You don't care what happens to us."

"Who says I don't?"

"You're not here. If you cared, you'd be here."

Karl took in a deep breath. "Danny, I care. I just can't live here anymore. It has nothing to do with you or Laura or Dee or anyone. It has to do with me. My mind doesn't work right when I'm here. To people back here I'll always be some snot-nosed kid who didn't really distinguish himself at Heiland High."

"Someone who made the Olympic team," Danny reminded him. "That's something nobody else in this town can say. Not even in hockey."

"Don't you see. I failed. I didn't even race in the Olympics."

"Doesn't matter, Karl. Everybody back here was so proud of you. They just didn't know how to say it to you when you came home. Everyone still tells me how great you were. That's hard to live with, ya know. I've never done anything like that. Never will."

Not knowing what to say, Karl simply shook his head. He had no idea anyone even considered him anymore.

Danny pulled himself to his knees with great difficulty. "Can we go in now. I got this nose thing here. I'm bleeding all over my jersey."

Karl helped his brother to his feet.

"And about that fedora," Danny said. "Not a lot of guys can pull that look off. But it works for you."

The two of them headed off toward the warming house.

•

Later that afternoon, Karl got a call from his mother at Dee's place. She wanted to meet him at the family graveyard.

Karl stood in the cold, his body stiffening by the minute. Clouds had moved in and there was a slight wind biting his skin like tiny needles poking in a hundred places on his face simultaneously. The gravestones were mostly covered with drifted snow.

His mother approached, her boots squeaking in the hard-packed snow.

They stared at each other for a moment, Karl wondering what she wanted at the graveyard.

He broke the silence. "It'll be months before the ground thaws enough to bury Uncle Jack and Geoffrey."

"Doesn't it smell fresh?" she said.

"Mom. My nostrils are frozen shut."

"You'd spend hours out in this cold. Skiing that little hill above the river. I couldn't get you inside. I worried so much that you'd fall and freeze to death."

"I was moving too much to feel it." Karl shuffled his feet in the snow waiting for his mom to speak.

"So. Your Uncle Jack might have been your father."

"What?"

She turned and started to walk away, but then stopped and turned toward him again.

"What can I say? We were young. A moment of weakness."

Smiling ever so slightly, she turned and shuffled off through the snow. Karl watched her, dumfounded. He couldn't think or move.

CHAPTER 21

THE DAWN OF MIDNIGHT

He would leave Heiland in the morning.

Karl sat quietly on Dee O'Brien's sofa, his laptop computer on, the fedora on his head, and his fingers clicking away at the keys.

They had stayed in Duluth at a hotel while the house was professionally cleaned. Karl had tried to get an earlier flight back to Germany, but there were only a few going to Frankfurt and they were booked. He had even considered skiing to take his mind off of everything, but dismissed it as a futile effort considering the conditions. The cold. The icy slopes. And the only skis available to him were those which he would never use again.

It was midnight now. He wore just a pair of sweats; no shirt, no socks. He continued with a story he had started a few days ago. He couldn't add to his novel. He was in the wrong place for that, the wrong frame of mind. The story he was writing was about a man who was haunted with a recurring dream. He was always in a squalid foreign street speaking a language he didn't understand. And they were violent dreams. He would wake in a cold sweat and remember vividly the dream but not be able to utter a word of the foreign language. Perhaps even worse, his waking memory was only a month long.

Karl stopped typing for a second. He looked at the black computer carrying case lying on the sofa next to him, and needed to see the photograph of Angelique Flaubert once again. He unzipped the pocket and produced the photo. Angelique stood next to him, her arm around his waist, his arm around her shoulder, both smiling warmly. He wondered if she had gone back to Brussels for the weekend. Had she succumbed to her parents and fiancé? He thought of calling her, seeing if she was home. But was he even certain she felt the way he did? He knew there should be no guilt, yet there was. Angelique was engaged to another man, would be married in June to a man she didn't love. And that was perhaps the worst part. She didn't love the guy. It was his only glimmer of hope, his only mental sanctuary. He still had a chance.

He looked at the photograph again. Angelique knew his passion. Could describe it with unfailing words. She knew he would never be satisfied with mundane mediocrity or even the status quo that most would find endearing. Perhaps there was still time. He only hoped that dawn would give him the same strength and power of midnight.

He set the photo down and continued with his story.

After a while he felt he was being watched. He looked up toward the bedroom door and saw Dee leaning against the door frame. She wore just a tiny pair of black bikini underwear. Her firm breasts were bare and pointed upward, the nipples hard from the cooler air of the living room.

"What are you writing?"

He saved what he was working on, and set the fedora to the back of his head. "The story I started a few days ago. The one about the dreams."

She nodded and then sat on the sofa next to him. "Do you always work this late at night?" Then she smiled. "With the fedora?"

This was the first time she had actually equated writing with work. "Yes. In Germany I have to write late. Usually after midnight. The tours are during the day. We travel mostly in the evenings. I also go to the university for research during the day when I'm not on a tour. The nights are more quiet. Forgiving." He smiled at her and then added, "The fedora is a constant. If you do the same thing repeatedly, there's a certain continuity."

"It's sort of like good luck."

He laughed and she looked embarrassed. "I'm sorry," he said. "You have this purity to you, Dee. What you see is what you get. I love that about you."

She turned her head away. "I'm afraid I'm not always that straight forward."

She looked down at the computer case at the photograph, picked it up and studied it. "Who's this?"

He felt embarrassed. Like he had when his mother found a *Playboy* in his room when he was in high school. "She's a tour guide that works with me. Her name is Angelique Flaubert. She's Belgian."

She continued to look at the photo. "She's as beautiful as her name. Where was it taken?"

"That's interesting," he said, taking the photo

from her hands gently. He pointed to a spot down the mountain beyond Angelique and him. "There. That's the outskirts of Innsbruck. In fact, this is the same place I hurt my knee."

"You still ski there?" she asked, an incredulous look across her face.

"Yeah. You've got to face your fears to overcome them." He realized after he said it that he should live other parts of his life that way also.

She shivered. "I couldn't do it."

"When you love something with such force and passion, you'll do anything to make it happen," he said. "For a while I thought I could no sooner give up skiing, than give up breathing."

"And now?"

"Some things just aren't that important."

She nuzzled next to his shoulder and wrapped her arm around his biceps, her smooth flesh melded with hard muscle in a powerful caress. "Come back to bed," she said, her eyes peering up at his.

He thought for a moment. "Sure. I'll be there in a few minutes. Let me just check to see if I left a complete thought on my story. I hate to come back to a story in mid-sentence."

She got up, a triumphant smile on her face, and headed toward the bedroom.

"Wait," Karl said. "Do you think Bugs Bunny was bi-sexual?"

"Huh?"

"We know that Bugs was at least a cross-dresser."

"What?"

"Never mind. I'll be there in a few minutes."

She leaned around the door frame, one breast

pointing directly at him. "Don't be too long. I may have to start without you."

He smiled back at her, and then logged onto his computer and pulled up his dream story. Quickly flipping to the end, he looked over what he had written. His character had discovered that others around him had known him for only a month also. It was as if he had been born just thirty days ago, had gone through his childhood the first two weeks, adolescence in the third week, and now in the fourth week middle adulthood. At this rate he would be dead in a few weeks. But was time so much a factor over place? For his dreams, his midnight nightmares, were persistently violent and always in another place. A place he no longer knew. A place where his dreams led him and he couldn't escape. Couldn't conceive of ever escaping. And always in a foreign language.

He saved what he had and sat for a moment in the nearly dark room. He thought about what he had just written, and wondered if he was trying to tell himself something. Could his subconscious escape from his mind to his fingers as if some spirit had forced him to reach out for that which he knew in his heart to be true anyway?

Thinking of Heiland, Karl wondered how he had even forced himself to write anything in the past few days. But he wasn't there in Heiland really, he was back in his Munich apartment, on his old tattered sofa, a beer in front of him, and the fedora appropriately on his head.

Setting the fedora on the sofa, he slowly rose and went into the bedroom.

CHAPTER 22

A FLASH OF AUBURN

When it was time to leave for Germany, Karl had no desire to remain in the frozen Heiland. He stood in the upper level at the Duluth airport, his bag checked through downstairs, and his computer at his feet.

Dee O'Brien was standing next to him, dressed to the hilt, a subdued expression on a troubled face.

"You come home once in a while, eh?" she said softly, moving closer to him.

"Why don't you come to Europe," he said. "I'd show you around. You'd like it."

She gave him a big hug, and he squeezed her tightly in return. With her head against his chest, she said, "I don't belong there. Just like you don't belong here anymore. I think God made a mistake when you were born here. You skipped a few generations, and should've grown up with your Bavarian ancestors."

That's what Karl himself had thought for the past few years. Perhaps even before he crashed while skiing in Innsbruck prior to the Olympics, when the man had asked him where he was from and he had answered Bavaria.

"You take care of yourself," Karl said. He kissed her on the forehead, and she swiveled her head up so their lips met for a long moment.

His plane was called for boarding. Karl held her until everyone else had walked out into the tunnel. Then he turned to go.

"Wait. I have to tell you something, Karl."

He gazed back at her.

"I asked my friend Bud, the cop, to come over the first day you got here."

"What! Why?"

She shook her head and tears streaked her face. "I love you, Karl," she said, walking away, backwards. "I needed you. I still do." Then she turned and skirted down the stairs out of sight.

"But why?" he yelled to her.

Karl waited until he could see her below, hurrying toward the basement to her car. Then he strolled down the long tunnel toward the plane.

•

The plane ride had been uneventful with complete spans of placidity. Karl had always tolerated flying. Planes were merely an instrument of time. Something to speed up the life of a traveler and make it as though time and time alone were the only factor worth considering in a life that had grown longer anyway, yet was cherished more for that quantity than for any regard for quality. And speed had never had anything to do with quality.

Karl had noticed while circling to land in Munich that the Bavarian Alps had received a fresh dusting of snow, and he imagined himself gliding smoothly down the Zugspitze through the new powder. A foot of fresh powder. He would hold the tips of his skis tight together just above the surface of the snow, carving left and right. A spray of snow would fly up behind him as he snaked gracefully down the steep grade. The only trace that a human had been there would be the trail he left behind. He wondered if life would be the same way.

From the airport Karl took a bus, watching the city unfold for him as if for the first time. Past the Frauenkirche, the twin Gothic domed towers stretching to the sky as if two arms were reaching up for God. Past the idle flower market and the New Town Hall. Past the Residenz and now-unspectacular Hofgarten. Then he got off and walked the last six blocks to his apartment, if for no other reason than to reacquaint himself with his home. He passed the bakery a block from his apartment, where he could smell croissants and coffee. He paused for a minute at the park across from his place, where he sat so many times casting a dreamy gaze toward the jagged limestone mountains to the south and hoped for snow.

He walked up the familiar cobbled sidewalk in front of his apartment, the ancient lamp posts, black with gold trim, resting in the mid-morning haze.

Picking up his mail from his landlord on the first floor, he slowly ascended the stairs to his apartment, shuffling through the few pieces of correspondence. A bill, a letter from an American magazine, probably a rejection, and then the curious letter from Todd Stewart.

Once in his apartment, he gently placed the fedora back on his bedpost, sat on the sofa, his leather coat thrown to one side, and he pulled Todd's letter from the envelope. Todd would leave him notes frequently, but usually not in sealed envelopes. He checked the envelope again and noticed he hadn't sent it through the postal system. It was hand carried. And since Todd had been in Italy for at least five days, he must have delivered it the day after Karl flew to America. He unfurled the two folds and read the hand-written letter:

Dear Karl,

By the time you read this I'll be freezing my ass off in the Dolomites. But I'm glad I could be of assistance to you. I consider you a good friend, perhaps the best I've ever known. I was a bit apprehensive at the airport. I'm sorry for that. I was struggling with a bloody dilemma that could only be overcome by an all-night painting session in a state of utter and unadulterated inebriation. I'm certain you understand fully. So I rose this morning, or should I say pulled myself up by the britches, and made a Goddamn decision. I have to tell you this. I could no sooner go on with life as though nothing happened, than imagine life without your friendship. Which isn't to say that her friendship is meaningless. It's just different. I'm writing of course about Angelique. She's a special woman. Both the flower and the butterfly that flutters over it. She came to my room the night before last, just after you two had been together. We talked. I should say she talked. I listened. She was doomed with a decision that she knew she had to make. You know she doesn't love

Adrien. She could no sooner love him than her butcher. But her family seems to have some sort of control over her and she's not sure if she's strong enough to overcome their power. She feels she is dependent on them, at least monetarily anyway. I tried to explain that money isn't everything, and she agreed. But with money comes power. And she's afraid that her family has too much of both to ever allow a relationship with someone they didn't approve of. If you haven't figured out what in the hell I'm talking about, then perhaps I am painting a picture more like Picasso. She has this special sparkle in her eyes when she talks about you, or even when your name comes up in conversation. Only an idiot couldn't figure out she loves you, Karl. This is tough for me to say. You know how I feel more than anyone. But she does love you. You need to go to her. Make the first move. Don't sit by idly and find yourself in twenty or thirty years, plastered in an old chair in front of the telly, wondering what could have been or what should have been. Well, I think I've said quite enough. Give me a call when I get back from Italy.

With the greatest respect,
Todd

When Karl finished reading and re-reading portions of the letter, he gently set it down on the coffee table. He let out a deep breath and then pulled out the picture of himself and Angelique on the Innsbruck mountain. He smiled as he ran his finger across her face on the photograph. He wasn't an idiot. He had sensed what Todd wrote. But the difference between foresight and true knowledge is always more clear after the fact.

He needed to talk with Todd to find out the exact words Angelique had used, but he wouldn't return from Italy for another three days. And by then Karl would be on his tour of Austrian and Swiss cities with Angelique, not knowing how he should proceed. Feeling as passionately as a man possessed to act, he knew he should take the chance and discard caution for action.

Sun seeped in through the window and seemed to draw Karl's eyes toward it. Kafka's fedora was there on the bedpost waiting for him to pick up and put on his head. He did just that. When he slowly set it on his head, he felt this great resurgence. A power. He knew it was stupid to raise an inanimate object to status of life and thought and feeling, but sometimes it was important to bring reverence where none should be. And who was to say that he was wrong for feeling something?

Jet lag was beginning to make him shake, but he couldn't sleep. It was nearing noon and he wondered where Angelique would be. He picked up the phone and called her, but hung up just as the phone rang for the third time. He wasn't sure why. Perhaps he wanted to meet her in person.

He freshened up a bit, splashing water in his face and combing his hair. Unknowingly, he put the fedora back on his head and hurried out the door.

The sun glimmered across the fresh snow cover. The streets and sidewalks were already clear and wet from the melted snow. He glance toward the Alps off in the distance and envisioned himself gliding down through that new snow again. He smiled at the thought, and then felt the pain in his knee as he took each step.

He shuffled slowly along the cobblestone sidewalk and imagined the feet that had smoothed the stones. Perhaps Kafka himself as a young student had strolled this very spot dreaming of a man who awoke in the body of an insect. But then the war had probably ensured that dream was doomed. For all he knew the stones could have come from across the river after the bombing had ended and restoration begun.

Continuing on, the university now in sight, he wondered if Angelique had made the trip to Brussels over the weekend. Maybe her family, or even Adrien, had convinced her for good that the marriage should continue as planned. And she would only be the biggest fool in Brussels if she didn't see the inevitability of the joining.

When he reached her apartment building across from the university, he stood for a minute below the steps as he had the last time he was with her, where they had actually kissed on the lips for the first time. First time, he thought, as if confident there would be more.

He eased up the steps, his knee clicking with pain.

After he got to the third floor, he hesitated briefly trying to form the words he wanted to say in his mind.

He knocked and waited. Nothing.

He knocked again. Nothing.

Somewhat dejected, he went outside and down the brick stairs to the sidewalk. He began to walk back toward his apartment, and then for some reason turned and crossed the street toward the university. He remembered sitting languidly at his usual wooden table in the foreign book section of the university library, watching Angelique move gracefully in front of him over the top of his book week after week. The words he read became more and more blurred as she slid each book in and out of the shelf as if caressing each volume. She would turn through the pages provocatively, run a long finger down the page, and then stop with an accusatory point and assured smile.

Inside the library, he said good afternoon to the old librarian who knew him well, and then took his normal seat after pulling a tattered version of Joyce's *Dubliners* from the shelf. He thought again of Angelique and the times he had watched her move among the shelves. The lights from above would shimmer off her auburn hair and seem to give the air around her head a soft red glow. He imagined touching the hair, then wrapping his hands among its thickness. Her lips would unknowingly mouth the words slightly as she read. And he thought of how those lips would feel against his. How they had felt once. They were full, engorged lips with a natural red from the blood of a passionate heart. Her piercing eyes would flow smoothly back and forth across the words, devouring each as a piranha scoops up its prey.

Once, in those first few weeks as he came to know every move she made, he had stood close enough to actually savor her perfume. It was an unobtrusive yet overwhelming flavor that he had stored neatly in his olfactory bulb only to be released or called up again each time she was near. Later when they had met at work and become friends he had found out the type of perfume and bought her a large bottle for her birthday. He wanted to ensure that she would never run out and change to an unfamiliar blend, setting his memory in some cataclysmic spin.

Karl slowly paged through *The Dead* as if the words would somehow magically drift from the page to his mind. He flipped to the end of the story and began to read of Gabriel's discovery of his wife and himself. He didn't want to find himself in Gabriel's fate. The week at his former home had proven that. He couldn't let his fictional dream escape into an oblivion that was normal and expected. A world in which complacency and acquiescence were synonymous with the wishes of those who wouldn't matter after death.

When he finished the story, he saw a flash of auburn above his book as if a ghost-like shape were floating through the tall shelves. Then again. The shape came closer and stopped as she had so many times in the past. She slid a book from the shelf and slowly flipped through the pages. She stood less than twenty feet away now, her hair glimmering from the lights. He took in a deep breath through his nose trying to capture her essence, but he couldn't. Then he gazed intently at her as if attempting to summon her mind to turn her head in his direction.

Finally, as if he had actually accomplished something, Angelique turned her face gently toward his. She smiled, walked immediately toward him, and took a seat across the table from him.

CHAPTER 23

EMERGENCE

Something had made her turn, but she wasn't sure what. He had sat at that table so many times, looking up cautiously from his book, watching her move from shelf to shelf and book to book, before they had officially met. Their eyes would meet for a moment and then quickly divert away as if they had truly locked in place by mere chance. She had noticed the books he read, left behind on the table after he had departed, and she would pick them up and run her hands over the binding and flip through the pages in an effort to understand the man that read them. The handsome American is how she had described him to the other tour guides. She knew even then that she would have to meet him at some point, if for no other reason than to hear his voice and listen to him articulate that which he read so fervently. She felt his presence deep within her, knowing that he would somehow change her in a positive way.

And now, sitting across from him again, as they had so many times in the past, she found herself changed in a more profound way than even she could have imagined. She smiled and gently set her hand on his.

"I'm so glad you returned," she whispered. "How was Minnesota?"

"Cold. Crazy. They all seemed like strangers."

Her eyes diverted away from his to the fedora on his head. "I see you're wearing the fedora."

He shifted his eyes up, and then quickly took off the hat and set it on the table. "I forgot I was wearing it."

"I was hoping you'd call when you got to the airport so I could come and get you."

"I wasn't sure if you'd gone to Brussels for the weekend and decided to stay longer."

She shook her head. "No. I shouldn't have gone. But, in a way, I'm glad I did."

"I just came from your place," he said. "I thought we should talk. Could we go somewhere else?"

She nodded and rose. They went outside and started walking down the sidewalk in the direction of her apartment. They were holding hands but didn't speak until they reached the road in front of her apartment building.

She looked at him and said, "Let's go to my place."

Unlocking the door, they went into her apartment. She hung her coat up and then asked for his leather jacket. As she adjusted the soft black leather over the hanger, she seemed to linger longer than normal with each sleeve until it was perfectly centered. Then she led him into the living room.

"Please have a seat," she said. "Would you like coffee or a beer?"

"A beer, thanks." He sat on the sofa, took off the fedora, and set it on the coffee table in front of him.

She returned with two beers and took a seat next to him on the sofa. She had been back from Brussels for two days, sitting much as she was now, wondering how forward she could be, how much she could tell him. It wasn't as though she had difficulty talking with him. Quite the opposite was true. Karl listened better than anyone she had ever met. He would watch her lips utter each word as if he were spelling them letter by letter with the movement.

Carefully he watched her every move. He thought of all the hours they had spent together at the Steinhaus discussing his writing and her art. Discussing the tours they had given, and those they were about to give. She understood better than anyone else his passion for skiing and his desire to write. She knew better than anyone that the pain in his knee was merely a constant reminder of the failure he felt over a lost dream. A dream that would haunt him forever.

Finally, he said, "Tell me about Brussels."

She shifted and made herself more comfortable on the sofa. "My father considers my marriage to Adrien a great business deal. A merger. My mother wants me to be some debutante like her. Dress up pretty, go to all the parties, and stick my nose into the air over anything that isn't suitable to her or her friends. Adrien's parents have been married so long they seem to share a brain. It's ridiculous. They want their son to marry before he gets any balder, or before anyone has a chance to see who he really is—a clone of his father. They have a shrewd business,

I'll give them that much. But I really can't see myself fitting in to their little plan."

Karl felt relief with those last words. "Is the marriage—"

"Canceled!" she said, with a quick release of air. "I thought my father would strangle me. My mother couldn't understand giving up a life of relative luxury."

"What are you giving up?"

"That's the point. Nothing. Adrien thinks he loves me, but he doesn't even know me. He thinks my painting is a cute little hobby. Something to pass the time. He could never understand my passion for it like you do. I've tried to explain it to him, but it was like explaining trigonometry to an infant."

Karl laughed aloud and she joined in. Their laughter finally slowed and he gently touched away her tears.

In a moment he said, "My parents think some demon has possessed me, twisted my mind like a pretzel, and left only my shell to walk the face of the Earth in a zombie-like state where passion is apropos of lust and love is saved for inanimate objects. They had always thought of my skiing as simply a distraction from growing up. Something that had gotten in my way of reality. It could never be anything else to them, you see, because only those things with languid and conventional respectability would fit into their idea of responsible living. And now I'm a writer. That would be fine if I were employed by some computer company writing boring technical manuals, or even pumping out dreary, overdone articles for some magazine or newspaper.

But, my God, to write fiction. How in the hell could that be respectable, or even remotely profitable? Writers are self-deprecating loners who drink themselves to death at a young age."

They stared at each other for a moment. It wasn't an uncomfortable moment, but one of discovering anew the features of each other's face; the deep eyes that refracted back to uncharted souls; the soft, moist lips that would breathe pleasure, and the lines at the corners of mouth and eyes that would only get deeper and deeper from enjoyable laughter.

"What about friends? Your brother and sister?"

"My brother is divorced and hates his job and life. My sister's husband ran off with a man. My cousin blew his brains out in front of me. And then my mother tells me my real father might have been my Uncle Jack. To top it off, I was duped by my best friend back there. Other than that, it was a wonderful trip."

She stared at him in wonder. "My God. I thought my trip was bad."

With a quick gulp he finished the last of his beer. He could no longer hold back his feelings. "Angelique, I want you to know how I feel about you."

She gazed at him carefully, wanting to stop him so she could speak first, but wanting even more to hear his words.

He continued. "I've known since the first time I saw you drift across my path in the library that there was something special about you. Something I would never overcome in this world. Something that would eventually penetrate my heart so fiercely I would never recover. Well, I was right." He paused for a moment to glance at the fedora. "My feelings for you have gotten stronger with each moment I see you, with each moment we are apart. I could never imagine you going off to Brussels with Adrien. Never dream of you being anything less than what you are now. I only hope you can find passion in your heart for me as I have for you."

She set her beer on the table and slid closer to him. "Shut up and kiss me!"

She pressed her lips gently on his and they slowly embraced.

After a moment she eased back from him and said, "Why do you think I spent so many hours in the library? In hope of seeing you. I tried to get there at the same time every Saturday. I asked Todd to invite you skiing. Then when you came to work for Bavarian Tours I couldn't believe my luck. The last year has been so difficult for me. We could see each other, talk with each other, dream each other's dreams, but that was all. My freedom was a bondage that I hadn't agreed to. And I had only fear of my parents and the wrath of propriety to blame. The night before you went home for your uncle's funeral I felt like we had something together that would never be changed even if I had married Adrien. I would have dreamt of you as he and I had sex. I wanted you at whatever cost, and I feared that you would return to America and never come back. I would never see you again but in my dreams. So I went to Todd after you had dropped me at my doorstep. I cried and told him how I felt about you in hope that he was such a friend to overcome his own feelings and find it in his heart to tell you. I wanted to find the strength to tell you myself, but that strength had alluded me until after I returned from Brussels—after I had told my parents, his parents, and Adrien to his face, that I couldn't marry him. You had talked about doing the right thing, that which was in my heart. Such a great weight has been lifted from my shoulders. It's indescribable. It's fate. I know it."

She had tears in her eyes, but she laughed anyway.

They could no longer help themselves. They embraced again, kissing passionately. She quickly unbuttoned his shirt while he pulled her sweater over her head. In a furious and frenzied fit of pure hunger, they discovered their nakedness for the first time. Their hearts raced as they breathed heavily the essence of each other. Nothing could separate them now.

•

In the morning there was a knock at Angelique's door. Karl answered it, wearing only his underwear.

Standing in the hall was Angelique's mother, a smile on her face. Next to her was a shocked Adrien.

"Is Angelique home?" her mother asked.

Karl was about to answer, when Angelique came out of her bedroom wearing only his T-shirt that stretched down to her thighs, and the fedora on her head.

"Karl, is someone at the . . . Mother! What are you doing here?"

Adrien tromped into the room and pointed at Karl. "Who's this?"

Angelique's mother pulled at Adrien's sleeve.

"Adrien, shut up and go to the car."

"But—"

"Go!" she demanded.

Karl closed the door behind Adrien, and then turned toward Angelique's mother. "Can I get you some coffee or tea?" he asked her.

"She's leaving," Angelique said emphatically.

"This is who you take instead of security," her mother said. "I see his assets. But—"

"I love him."

Her mother shifted her eye's from Angelique to Karl and then back to her daughter. "I can see that in your eyes."

"Doesn't that mean anything?"

Her mother went to the door. "If you need anything, I'm always there. After I explain things to your father, bring him home with you. I'm sure Eliza will approve as well."

She opened the door to leave.

"Please stay," Angelique said.

"No. I'll be explaining this to Adrien all the way to the airport. Probably the flight too. It was nice meeting you, Karl. You two put some clothes on. You'll catch a cold."

With that, she left the two of them standing and staring at each other. Then they both start laughing.

"That went well," Karl said.

"Yeah."

CHAPTER 24

ASCENSION

The Mercedes bus glided along the autobahn from Vienna toward Innsbruck in no great hurry. It was midnight and nearly seven hours before they had to check in at their hotel.

Karl and Angelique had spent the last few days guiding the two groups of American and British tourists to all of Vienna's high points. That evening they had hosted a dinner at a fine restaurant and then brought them to a production of the Boys' Choir and a Mozart concerto. The two buses were waiting for the groups outside the concert hall and had whisked them away to the autobahn. It would be the only time during the tour they would travel at night and sleep on the bus, since they were essentially retracing the route they had previously taken from Salzburg.

Now in the front seat of the bus, alone, Karl clicked away at his laptop computer in the darkness. He couldn't see his screen, but then he didn't need to.

Fritz would glance over his shoulder from time to time to see if he was still awake. But Karl couldn't fall asleep now. He kept his eyes trained on the bus in front of him, the bus of tourists Angelique was guiding.

He thought of the two buses linked together, each moving in unison to the next city, much like he and Angelique had been since he returned from America. First, there had been the two nights in Munich before the tour began, where they had spent each moment together, making love and simply connecting with the presence of the other. Then the night in Salzburg, where Karl had discreetly sneaked down to Angelique's room to stay. And the two nights in Vienna, where she had come to his room.

Now was the first night without her. Yet, he felt her presence even from the short distance between the two buses.

He picked up the radio microphone and keyed it.

"Angelique?" he said quietly.

"Yes, what's wrong?" she said softly through the small speaker.

"Nothing. Just wanted to hear your voice."

"Me too."

He set the microphone down and closed up his computer, setting it under his seat. He leaned back and drew the fedora down over his eyes. He thought about fate and the fedora and Angelique as the bus droned on into the darkness.

Printed in the United States
1328600001B/42